Perfect Girl

Also
by
Mary
Hogan

THE SERIOUS KISS

Mary Hogan

HarperTempest
An Imprint of HarperCollins Publishers

HarperTempest is
an imprint of HarperCollins
Publishers. • Perfect Girl
Copyright © 2007 by
Mary Hogan • All rights
reserved. Printed in
the United States of
America. No part of
this book may be used
or reproduced in any
manner whatsoever without
written permission except in
the case of brief quotations
embodied in critical articles and
reviews. For information address
HarperCollins Children's Books, a
division of HarperCollins Publishers,
1350 Avenue of the Americas, New York,
NY 10019. www.harperteen.com Library
of Congress Cataloging-in-Publication
Data available ISBN-10: 0-06-084108-7
— ISBN-13: 978-0-06-084108-9 Typography
by Sasha Illingworth 1 2 3 4 5 6 7 8 9 10
❖ First Edition

For Bob,
forever

Acknowledgments

ETERNAL THANKS TO THE AMAZING Amanda Maciel, who's truly more of a writing *partner* than an editor. This book would not be this book without you. My love and appreciation to Laura Langlie, the best agent ever, and the many incredible New York women who inspired the character Martine: Dr. Joy Browne, Joanna Patton, Antonia van der Meer, Carol Tuder, Jo-Ann Robotti, Leslie Monsky, Florence Isaacs, Su Robotti, Karen Walden, Rosemarie Lennon, Susan Kane, Kathy Green, Susan Sommers, Linda Konner, and, New Yorker in spirit, Julie Hogan.

Perfect Girl

SHE WALKS INTO CLASS TEN MINUTES AFTER THE BELL.
Twenty heads turn. Forty eyes watch her walk up to the
front with her perfectly tan legs, perfectly blue halter top,
and perfectly sweeping bangs.

Mr. Roland is already boring us. Chalk dust flying, he
lists the six member councils of the United Nations on the
board. His short-sleeve white shirt is so thin you can see the

shadow of his back hair.

" . . . General Assembly, Security Council . . . ," his nasal voice drones on.

"I'd like to member her council," one of the guys says, flicking his head at the new girl. The class erupts in laughter. Well, the *boys*, anyway.

"Oh my," Mr. Roland says, turning around. "Who do we have here?"

She hands him a note. I stare and twirl a strand of red hair around my finger.

"Take a seat," our teacher says. And the new girl does. She calmly walks to the back of the room without blushing though everyone is watching her every move. Especially Perry. *My* Perry.

"This is Jenna Wilson, everyone," says Mr. Roland. The boys nod and smirk. The girls bend their lips up in fake smiles. Jenna sits and faces front. I notice she has a French manicure on her fingers and her toes. Curling my ragged nails into my palms, I face front, too.

" . . . Economic and Social Council, International Court of Justice . . . "

Mr. Roland returns to the chalkboard and blathers on. The way he has all semester. I hear with my ears, but my mind is on the new girl. The *perfect* girl, who now sits between me and Perry Gould. I feel him checking her out. My heart sinks.

Of all times, why *now*?

"DUCK."

That's the first word I ever heard him say. The one I remember, anyway. It came flying over the chain-link fence that separates our two backyards. He might have been identifying the airborne rubber duck, or telling me to get out of the way. Who knows? What I do know is this: From word one, Perry Gould and I have been friends. *Best* friends, probably. But don't tell my other best friend, Celeste.

Perry still lives on Fifth Street in Odessa, Delaware; I still live on Sixth. We've been connected all our lives by geography. Now, I'm hoping for some anatomical connection, too.

"Duck," I'd repeated as a little kid, tottering over to retrieve the yellow rubber bird in my backyard.

Perry's mom sunned herself on a lawn chair beside their wading pool. My mother was on her hands and knees, planting herbs in our vegetable garden.

Mrs. Gould shouted, "Sorry!" Then she asked, "Want to come swimming, Ruthie?"

Of course I did. But Mom's forehead got all creased with thoughts of bacteria, drowning—

"I won't take my eyes off her, Fay," said Mrs. Gould.

Reluctantly, Mom let me go next door.

"I'll get her bathing suit and the sunscreen," she said, grunting as she got up.

By the time she returned, however, I was through the gate, stripped down to my underpants, and splashing Perry in his pool. That was our first date. Perry saw me topless when being topless didn't mean a thing. We played together long before life complicated every touch.

"What do you think it stands for?" Celeste asks me after social studies class. "Jennifer?"

"Wouldn't that be *Jenni* instead of *Jenna*?" I say.

4

"Wasn't the president's daughter named Jenna?" my second-best friend, Frankie, asks. Her real name is Frances, which actually suits her better since she's shy and round and a bit of a follower. Unlike Celeste, who charges forward into every situation not caring who she plows over.

Celeste won't admit it, but she's a bit of a Frances inside. And I see myself in both of them. Probably the reason we all get along. Most of the time.

"I thought her name was Barbara," Celeste says. "After her grandmother."

"That's the other one," I say. "They were both named after their grandmothers. Which is why I got a B on that Constitution quiz. My brain is full of useless trivia about twins."

Celeste says, "God, I hope she's not a twin."

"Me, too," I say, sighing.

"Me, three," Frankie says.

We silently walk across the grass to our lunch spot. I hurry to get in the shade. The last thing I need is another freckle. My long red hair is already frizzing in the afternoon humidity. Celeste plops down in the direct sun, twists her straight black hair into a knot, and tilts her face skyward. Frankie rolls her tight capri pants up over her knees and kicks off her flip-flops. I notice that she forgot to rub self-tanning cream on the tops of her feet.

As we open our bag lunches, I know my friends are thinking what I'm thinking: *Isn't freshman year hard enough without a new girl? A perfect girl?*

"Besides," Celeste says, her eyes closed, "who comes to a new school right at the end of the year?"

"Yeah," says Frankie. "Who?"

"Maybe her parents are fugitives," I suggest.

"Delaware's Most Wanted," Celeste says, laughing.

Frankie asks, "Do you think their pictures are in the post office?"

There she is across the lawn. She's heading straight for us. Her long, light-brown hair flips right and left with each step. Her thigh muscles flex as she walks down the hill. Already, she's been swallowed up by the Semi-Populars. Two girls from the soccer team are showing her around. My pulse races as they get close, but they pass our tree without acknowledging us at all. Not that we look like we care. Celeste glances at her, then closes her eyes again. Frankie takes a bite of her peanut butter sandwich. Me, I flip my hair and pretend I don't notice her deep dimples or the way her eyes crinkle when she laughs. *At least she's not blond,* I think. Thank God for small favors.

"Hey."

My heart flutters as I hear a familiar voice behind me.

"Hey, Perry," I say, flipping my hair again, turning around. Perry nods at me, but I see his eyes shift to *her.* To my horror, she looks right at him and smiles. Crud. Now he's seen her deep dimples, too.

Celeste opens one eye and scoffs.

"If it isn't P. Nerdy in his gangsta pants."

"It's just Nerdy now," Frankie says. "He dropped the P."

"God, you guys," I say, glaring at my friends. Then I squint and look up at the boy I'm inexplicably ga-ga over. The only boy who's seen me topless and knows all my secrets. Perry bobs his head to the hip-hop music in his ears. He wears a gigantic white T-shirt over huge, hem-frayed jeans. Admittedly, it *is* a tad lame. Especially the wool hat when it's, like, ninety degrees. But Perry will try anything not to look like the science nerd he is—even fronting like a rapster.

"You're not fooling anyone," I told him a million times. Perry looks smart eating corn flakes in the morning. He's going to be an astronaut. The astronomy class at Liberty High was created for him and the other brains who are so far beyond ninth grade science it's not even funny. Perry's idea of the perfect vacation is a shuttle flight to the Space Station. I mean, come *on*.

At school, though, Perry pretends he's a boy from the 'hood without a stratospheric GPA. I used to think he was out of his mind. Now, when I look at him, I feel like I'm going out of mine.

"We're *busy*," Celeste says to Perry, all snotty. "Try not to trip on your pants when you leave, Bozo."

"Try not to confuse your age with your I.Q.," Perry says to Celeste, nodding at me again, then pimp-walking away.

"Later!" I say to Perry, wincing at how desperate I

sound. Annoyed, I ask Celeste, "Why do you have to be so mean to him?"

"He's mean to *me*."

"You were mean first."

"What, are we in kindergarten? Who cares about Perry? It's not like he's your boyfriend, Ruthie," Celeste says. "It's not like I *have* to like him."

I swallow. "He is my friend."

"Your *sympathy* friend. Just because you were friends as kids doesn't mean you need to be friends now."

What could I say? I didn't have the guts to tell my best friend that I was officially in love with Perry Gould. She can't see into his poet's soul the way I suddenly can. And if I told Frankie about my new thing for Perry, she'd instantly blab to Celeste. Which is why Frankie will always be best friend number *two*.

Most of all, neither one of my friends would understand what happened last Friday night. Particularly since I don't understand it myself.

IT WAS DELICIOUSLY WARM OUT, ONE OF THOSE PRE-summer nights that makes you crazy because school is almost over, but finals are still ahead. It's like you're dying to be free but you can't let go. Not yet.

"Check this out," Perry said.

We were up on the flat part of his roof—like we always were—hanging out. Perry was staring at the stars through the monster telescope his mother saved for two years to buy him. It was tilted toward the black sky, standing on its tripod. Me, I was thinking about how your whole life can be formed by an accident. Not in the "car wreck" sense. In the "not on purpose" sense. Like, where you live. And the fact that a totally abnormal life has to be *your* life because that's all you were given.

"Ruthie, check this out," Perry repeated.

"It better be good," I said. Stars, to me, are a waste of time. Unless, of course, we're talking about Orlando Bloom.

Crouching down, I pressed the eyepiece up to my face.

"See it?" Perry asked, excited.

"I see a white dot."

"That's it!" He stepped closer to me. "Vega! It's the brightest star in the Summer Triangle."

I looked, shrugged.

"Can you see Epsilon Lyrae right next to it?" he asked. "Can you?"

What, I was looking for *two* dots now? Pulling my eye away from the telescope, I asked Perry, "Do you ever wonder how totally different you'd be if you lived in Alaska or California or New York?"

"It's a *double* star, Ruthie," he said. "You can't always see it."

"That's what I'm saying! How can you see who you really are when you're stuck in someone else's life?"

Perry rolled his eyes. We'd had this discussion before.

The two of us were trapped in a maternal noose. Both only children. Both dadless. Perry's father ran off with a shiatsu massage therapist from Dover when he was two. My dad . . . well, he never *was*. Mom chose me the way you pick sheets.

"I'd like green ones to match the bedspread. Make sure they're the right size because they have to fit what I already have."

My mother selected my red hair and blue eyes to match her own. She chose a dad who was in college, because she never went. I had a little heart disease in my paternal genes, she told me, but no more than the average person.

Average person. How could I ever be average when my father was only a sperm in a syringe?

"No child was wanted more than you," Mom said. It took two expensive tries at the fertility clinic in Wilmington for me to take. "Why else would I go to so much trouble?"

My mom has lived in tiny Odessa, Delaware, all her life. Population: 286. Before I was born (Population: 285), my mom worked at the only diner in town.

"I knew everyone," she told me. "No one was interested in me."

My question is this: If Mom had waited, would a stranger have stopped by Taylor's Diner? Someone who hadn't known her all his life and decided she was the *one*? Was a normal dad only a breakfast special away?

Perry feels it, too. That *fizzing*. Like club soda in your

11

veins. A constant reminder that you're not like everybody else. Not enough to take over your whole life, but enough to nag at you and keep *normal* just out of reach.

I'm not naive. I know nobody is completely normal. Even when people look and act normal, they aren't normal deep down. But they probably have a moment when they *feel* normal. When they buy a Father's Day card without thinking twice about it, when their dads teach them how to drive, or walk them down the aisle. They have family stories and photos and Christmas mornings that are littered with torn wrapping paper. They don't feel like their mothers would shrivel up and die without them.

It's those little moments that add up to a family. When your dad isn't around, you don't know exactly what you're missing. You just know it's something big.

Most of the time, I stop my mind from dwelling on it. Because when I do, I stress out. Did my mother ever once consider what her decision might mean to me? Did it occur to her that a girl needs a dad so she can grow up to understand boys?

"If you look carefully, Ruthie, you'll see something truly amazing," Perry said last Friday night on top of his roof. "The two stars of Epsilon Lyrae are actually *double* stars as well."

Peering through the telescope, I could feel his breath on the back of my neck, his warm hand on my shoulder.

"Epsilon is a double-double star. Can you see it? Can

you see all four of them? They're awesome. You've got to see them."

I stared until four dots came into focus. "Oh."

"You see them?"

Perry's forehead pressed lightly against the back of my head. It felt totally familiar, but somehow, completely new.

Yeah, I saw them.

"Aren't they awesome?" he asked.

"They are." For the first time, I meant it.

"Do you realize you're looking at massive nuclear reactions held together by gravitational force?"

I hadn't.

"*Astronaut* means *space sailor*," he said almost dreamily. "That's what I want to be—a space sailor."

We both fell silent, imagining Perry sailing into space, seeing Earth as a beach ball, feeling like a small dot.

I pulled away from the telescope, slightly dizzy. Then I gazed at Perry's face. It was like I'd never truly seen him before. I could hardly catch my breath. His jaw was angular. His brown freckles had faded. Were his eyelashes always long and curly? He had sideburns, sort of. And one crooked tooth. Why had I ever thought it looked goofy? And was he always so tall? All of a sudden, I noticed that Perry had grown into his face and body. They weren't overtaking him anymore. He looked . . . *cute*. It took all my energy to keep from reaching my hand up to make sure he was real.

That's when it happened. *Thwang.* It was the steam

coming off his chest, his grasslike smell, the feeling that we were all alone—the two of us—on a tiny patch of roof in the middle of an infinite universe. Just us fatherless space sailors held together by gravitational force. As unexpected as a shooting star, I fell in love with my (almost) best friend.

"Some nights you can see the Ring Nebula," Perry said. "But not now. It's too early."

He was wrong. It was too *late*. I was weightless in his orbit. I would never view Perry Gould as my "pal" again. It was beyond my control. My heart knew it, my knees knew it.

If only I could figure out a way to let Perry in on the news. Before someone—like the new girl, the *perfect* girl— gets her French-manicured hands on my soon-to-be (*please* God!) boyfriend.

MOM HAS HER FEET PROPPED UP ON OUR OLD BURLED wood coffee table. Her purple velour pants stretch tightly across her thighs. She wears the slippers she calls her "inside shoes" and knits a baby blanket out of yellow yarn.

"Did you finish your homework?" she asks.

"I just walked through the door, Mom," I say. "Give me a break."

She gives me a *look*.

"Want a fish stick?" she asks. "I'm having a little afternoon snack."

"God, no."

"Will you get me another one, then? They're in the toaster oven."

My eyes bug out. "Have you been sitting there all day waiting for your servant to come home?"

Mom slides her glasses on top of her head. "As a matter of fact, Ruthie, you're twenty-two minutes late. You know how I worry when you dillydally."

Groaning, I dump my backpack on the matching wing chair beside my mother, which *doesn't* match because she tried to reupholster it herself and gave up when it looked all pinched, like it was wearing fabric belonging to a much smaller seat. Nothing in our house matches—not the road-kill-brown sofa with the olive-green-and-aqua afghan Mom knit (the wool was on sale), not the "neutral" area rug that long ago lost its neutral status, not the stack of flea market dinner plates in our kitchen cupboard that looks like a heap of pancakes about to topple over. Not even the curtains. One is a faded rose print, the other a plaid.

"Do you ever feel so totally stuck in your life it's like quicksand sucking you straight into hell?" I ask.

Mom—her kinky reddish-gray curls exploding from her head like old bed springs—blinks her eyes at me. I see her brain clicking. My heart races. Is it possible I'm going to have an honest, soul-baring moment with my mother?

"Don't forget the tartar sauce," she says.

Groaning even louder, I grab my pack and shout, "Hell!" Then I stomp out of the living room and up the stairs to my room.

How am I ever going to escape my fourteen-going-on-twelve existence and keep Perfect Girl away from Perry Gould and inspire him to stop viewing me as one of the guys if my only role model knits baby blankies for a living, and probably never even had sex?! The woman who's supposed to guide me into adulthood thinks hunger is nature's way of telling you how large your body was meant to be. She believes coloring your hair is "lying" and makeup is for clowns. Plus, she considers pop culture to be mind poison. We don't even have cable! I have to watch MTV at Celeste's house. My computer has a *dial-up* modem. We might as well be Amish!

She can get her own tartar sauce.

On my way up the stairs, I pass Mr. Arthur, the seriously ancient tenant who rents the third floor of our ramshackle house.

"Something smells yummy," he says.

"Hell, hell, hell, hell," I say with each step upstairs.

"What do you need help *with*?" he asks, completely mis-understanding me. "You know, when I was a boy . . . "

I groan even louder.

Mr. Arthur is a double threat—nearly deaf, yet unable to shut up. His white hair is in a constant state of bed-head, and the lenses in his glasses are so thick it looks like his eyes are peering out from the back of his head.

Once, I asked him if "Arthur" was his first name or his last name.

"Interesting story, that," he said.

Back then, I stifled my groans.

"My ancestors moved here before it was even called Odessa," he began, chuckling as if it were his own private memory. "They called it Cantwell's Bridge because this fellow named Cantwell built a bridge over the Appoquinimink Creek."

"Uh-huh."

"Our town was a hopping port. They shipped goods all along the Delaware River until the railroad came in and wrecked everything."

"Your name—?" I glanced at the door.

"To save the day, the town smarties changed the name to Odessa, after Odessa, *Russia*, of all places. Can you believe it?"

"Is Mom home?"

"They figured, since Odessa, Russia, was such a shipping powerhouse, Odessa, *Delaware*, would be, too. It would rub off, so to speak."

"I have homework."

"Of course, it didn't fly. The shipping trade faded away, the town fell apart, we ended up with a Russian name and a few fancy old houses that the rich folks turned into museums. The original homes are dumps."

Did he just call our house a dump? Not that he was wrong.

"Now Christmas in Odessa, that's another story. . . ."

Mr. Arthur prattled on. He'd be an interesting man if he wasn't so, you know, *boring.* He's lived with us since his wife died, which was forever ago. Almost all my life. He doesn't have any kids of his own. As far as I know, he doesn't have anyone but us.

Still, beneath his chatter and weirdness, I can tell he loves my mom and me. Which, admittedly, feels pretty good. And *nobody* loves our town like he does. Mr. Arthur is a fourth-generation native Odessan. Which is why he's the Grand Marshal in the upcoming Odessa Peach Blossom Parade, and has been ever since I can remember. On parade day, my mother and I will stand on the sidelines and cheer him on. I have to admit, seeing his face all lit up as he struts down Main Street makes me feel lit up, too.

I still don't know if "Arthur" is his first or last name.

Even my mother calls him Mr. Arthur, as does everyone else in our town. I guess I could ask someone, but no way am I going to ask him again.

Up in my room, I feel like I'm going to explode. How can life change so dramatically in one day? A month before summer vacation and the hottest thing in our school is *her*? Plus, I definitely saw eye contact and a grin. Without a doubt, Perry spotted those dimples. He's already thinking about Perfect Girl. I *know* he is! The last time Perry looked at me the way he looked at her was when he was musing about the solar system.

I'm skunked.

If you told me I had a week to ace the SATs, I'd hit the books and study. But how do you learn how to become a girl who makes boys pant when you're a totally *im*perfect virgin who knows nothing?

"Ruthie?" Mom calls me from downstairs.

Facedown on my bed, I say, "What?" into my mattress.

"Ruthie!"

"What?!" I turn my head and shout.

"I hope you're cleaning your room."

"I am," I lie. Then I pull a pillow over my head.

It's there—in the darkness of my fiber-filled bedding, breathing in the familiar smell of laundry detergent and shampoo—I realize I have only one choice. Mom is going to freak out. But I can't be in charge of her feelings. Not when I'm in love with a boy who has his eye on a girl whose hair is as naturally straight as her teeth. It's an *emergency.* I need major help. And there's only one woman who can give it: Aunt Marty.

AS LONG AS I LIVE, I WILL NEVER FORGET THE DAY I FIRST met my mother's sister.

I was eleven. My boobs were nonexistent, my freckles were out of control. I wore my favorite sundress without realizing what a geek I was. Until I got there . . . the city that changed my life.

Mom and I drove for *hours.* Actually, it was only about

four, but it felt like forty. We left our crumbly old house in Delaware on the morning before the Fourth of July. I remember the date because I consider it my independence day—the day I discovered who I was meant to be.

"Buckle your seat belt, Ruthie," Mom said that morning.

"It's buckled."

"Is it tight?"

"It's one size fits all."

Mom sighed. "Okay, then. Lock your door."

"It's locked."

"And roll up your window."

"Why? I'm hot."

My mother gaped at me. "Because something could fly in the window from the highway."

I gaped back. "Like what?"

"A bug, a chunk of gravel, a sharp piece of glass. Roll it up, Ruthie."

I rolled my *eyes* . . . then the window. We hadn't even left the driveway yet.

"Are you ready?" she asked.

"I can't wait," I said.

Off we went. Mom drove through Boyds Corner and Bear, past Wilmington. She stayed in the right lane, bit her lip each time a car came onto the turnpike. We ate pretzel sticks, listened to stupid oldies on the radio. Every two seconds, Mom tilted her head up and checked out the rearview.

"That car is following awfully close," she said, slowing down even more.

We crawled along the Pennsylvania border, up the length of New Jersey, stopping only once in Secaucus so Mom could steel herself for the tunnel ride into Manhattan.

"Mom!" I said, exasperated. "We're almost there!"

"I can't help thinking about that Sylvester Stallone movie," she said. "There's an explosion, and everyone gets trapped in the tunnel. Water rushes in and cars crash and people panic. I don't mean to scare you."

"You're not scaring me. That's just a movie."

"Just because something is fiction doesn't mean it can never be fact."

I sighed extra loud, stared out my closed window. "I think there's a bridge."

"A *bridge*? Didn't you see that Schwarzenegger film?"

Even at eleven years old, I knew my mother was nuts. Like the time Celeste's parents went on the coolest cruise ever and all my mom could say was, "Hello! Does the word *Titanic* mean nothing to those people?"

That's why I was shocked when she accepted Aunt Marty's invitation for a long weekend in New York. If we could only get there.

"Okay," Mom finally said in Secaucus, gripping the steering wheel. "Hold on, Ruthie. We're going in."

I clapped my hands, and my mother got back on the road. We inched along in traffic, behind a huge bus, around a giant looping ramp. Suddenly, I saw it: *Manhattan.* It seemed to spring up out of nowhere. The afternoon sun flickered off the skyscrapers. The whole city glowed pink. Blue water rippled in the wake of a bright white boat. How could so many buildings be packed onto such a tiny island? My pulse pounded. It was the most beautiful sight I'd ever seen.

Like a tropical waterfall, the sense that my life had changed washed over me. I mean, it was as real as a splash of water. I felt like I'd been sleeping for eleven years and just woke up.

"How many people live in those buildings?" I asked my mom in awe.

"Too many," she said.

Seeing Manhattan glistening on the water, hearing a ferry blast its horn, smelling car exhaust—they all filled me with an incredible longing. My head didn't understand it yet, but my heart felt it. That day was the beginning of my awareness that I was born into the wrong life.

Her knuckles white on the steering wheel, Mom nervously started singing, "Dah, dah, dah, dah, dahhhh." The "New York, New York" song. I looked at her and could not help but laugh. She laughed, too. And we both forgot about cinematic disasters and lives not lived . . . for a little while, at least.

WE MADE IT THROUGH THE TUNNEL INTO MANHATTAN
absolutely dry.

"Whew," Mom said, "that was close."

Again, I rolled my eyes. I felt like saying, "Just because
we drove through a tunnel that thousands of people drive
through every day doesn't mean we narrowly escaped
death." But I wasn't in the mood for one of Mom's "Death

and Destruction" lectures.

"Every thirteen minutes, someone dies in the United States from a car crash. Every *thirteen* minutes!"

I'd heard it a gazillion times before. My mother has a freakish memory for mortality statistics. That's probably why we still live in Delaware. Last time Mom checked, only twenty-one people had been murdered in a year.

"Because it's the smallest state in the U.S.!" I remember saying.

"The *second* smallest," Mom said. "But Rhode Island has more homicides!"

My mother hung a right on Forty-second Street and headed for the east side of Manhattan. I couldn't shut my mouth . . . literally. I was speechless, but I couldn't keep my jaw closed. There were so many people, so much color! Taxi yellow, neon pink, green, turquoise. It looked as though the buildings were alive and dancing against the sky.

"Help me watch for pedestrians," Mom said, still sweating. "They have no regard for cars here."

I watched for pedestrians, for celebrities, for homeless people, for the entire circus that whirled around us. I don't think my mother took a normal breath until she was at Aunt Marty's apartment clear across the island, near the East River, in a neighborhood called Sutton Place.

"We made it," she said, exhaling. There was no neon, no homeless people. The only humans I saw were doormen and women with little dogs and big black sunglasses.

Mom circled the block a couple of times, looking for a place to park. Finally, she gave up and pulled into a pay garage. She pulled right out, though, when they told her it would cost more than a hundred dollars to leave her car there all weekend. Circling again, Mom stopped in front of Aunt Marty's.

"Ask your aunt what I should do," she said, idling in front of a tall building with a long green awning. "She's in apartment twenty-two."

Before I could unlatch my seat belt, a door man appeared at the car door. He wore a navy-blue suit with gold buttons. Even though it was hot out, he wasn't sweating at all. He reached for my door with white-gloved hands. When I finally managed to get out, the doorman smiled and walked me into the building.

"My aunt is in apartment twenty-two," I said. "I need to ask her where my mom should park."

Nodding, he said, "Wait here." I watched him go back out to the curb and talk to my mother. He pointed his glove down the street, and Mom disappeared.

Aunt Marty's lobby was gorgeous. It smelled like roses and wood polish. The marble floor was so shiny I could see myself in it. There were two elevators, surrounded by brass.

"Mrs. Arenson, right?"

I blinked. Is it possible my mother never told me Aunt Marty's last name? Of course it was. I was already eleven, and I'd only seen her once before, when I was a baby.

Before I could figure out what to say, the doorman had Aunt Marty on the phone and she told me to "come on up."

"By myself?" I blurted out, channeling my mother for a moment.

"I'll go with you," the doorman said.

Together, we entered the elevator. Briefly, it occurred to me that Mom would flip out if she knew I got onto a New York elevator with a strange man. But he didn't seem strange at all. He seemed like the nicest man in the world.

"Are you here on vacation?" he asked on the way up.

"I guess so."

Honestly, I wasn't sure why we were there. Mom and her sister never had gotten along. Something had happened a long time ago that kept them apart. Mom refused to tell me what it was. And I had no idea what brought them together that weekend. All I knew was my aunt Marty was my only living relative—other than sperm dad's mystery family—and I was finally getting to see her when I was old enough to not have to wear diapers.

The elevator dinged, the door opened, and there she was.

"Ruthie?"

I tried to speak, but what do you say when you're suddenly transported into another world?

"Come in!" Aunt Marty held her arms open to me. The elevator opened directly into her apartment.

Aunt Marty thanked the doorman, and he disappeared

behind the closing elevator doors. Wrapping me in her arms, my aunt held me for a long time. If my mom had embraced me that long, I would have gasped for air and wriggled away. Aunt Marty's cocoon felt delicious.

"You smell nice," I said.

She loosened her grip and guided me into what I can only describe as a mansion in the sky. Everything was white—the couches, the marble floor (just like the lobby), the sunlight streaming through the windows that ran the length of one wall, from floor to ceiling. The only thing that wasn't white was the shiny black piano. Its lid was lifted, the keys polished.

"You *live* here, Auntie Martha?"

"Call me Aunt Marty," she said. Then she smiled the way I imagined a queen would smile when she peered down from her throne and knew, just *knew*, the whole kingdom belonged to her.

"No luggage?" Aunt Marty asked.

I tried to tell her that my suitcase was in the car, with my mother. But the view took my breath away. The river was a silver ribbon. We were so high above the city, the buildings looked like gray Legos.

"Sit down, sweetie."

"Here?" The white couch scared me. I was certain my dress would smudge it.

Aunt Marty laughed. "Would you rather sit on the floor?"

I laughed, too. Tried to look as casual as she did. I even tossed my head back, but it felt all jerky. Like someone had pulled my ponytail. Finally, I sat, awkwardly perched on the edge of the couch cushion.

My aunt tucked herself into the couch beside me. She pulled her knees up and draped one arm over the back. Everything about her was effortless. Unlike my mother, who huffed and puffed just getting in and out of the car. Aunt Marty's teeth were white without being fake white, her smooth skin seemed to glow from inside.

"I'm so happy to finally look at your face," she said. She reached up and touched my cheek, and I instantly felt pretty.

"Iced tea?" she asked.

I nodded.

"Three iced green teas, please, Renata!" Aunt Marty called over her shoulder. Then she looked at me and winked. "Assuming your mother hasn't driven back to Odessa by now."

AUNT MARTY REFUSED TO TAKE US TO THE STATUE OF
Liberty, the Empire State Building, or Times Square.

"That's not the real New York," she said that day.

Instead, we walked across the Brooklyn Bridge and ate
custard ice cream. We shopped for clothes in the Back
Room at Loehmann's, then for shoes at Barney's.

"Do you have these in red?" she asked the salesman, picking up a pair of shoes on the *display* table instead of the clearance rack. "Fay, is this heel too high for Odessa?"

After seeing Mom's toes, Aunt Marty insisted on manis and pedis. (Though, of course, Mom only let me get clear polish.) When our nails were dry, we strolled through Central Park.

"*Never* a carriage ride!" Aunt Marty shuddered.

Mom refused to go into the subway because she read that a crazy guy once pushed a woman onto the tracks. "I also heard that an air conditioner fell out of a penthouse apartment and killed a pedestrian," she said, looking up.

"Well, *that* wasn't cool," Aunt Marty replied.

I burst into laughter and would have thrown my arms around my aunt if Mom hadn't glared me into immobility.

After a late lunch at some tiny café where the chef came out and kissed Aunt Marty's cheek, we meandered through the Museum of Modern Art.

"Isn't that—?" I stopped in my tracks as we turned a corner in the museum and saw one of the most recognizable paintings ever.

"*Starry Night*," Aunt Marty said. "Van Gogh's masterpiece."

I stared at the swirls of blue and green and couldn't believe I was inches away from something so famous.

"He painted this purely from memory, since he'd

checked himself into an asylum at the time. See how the circles surround each yellow star? It's as if his spirit was trapped inside, caught in a whirl of emotions."

I beamed. Aunt Marty knew *everything*.

"Plus," Mom said, one eyebrow cocked as if she had the inside scoop, "van Gogh is the artist who cut off his own ear for the woman he loved."

"Only *part* of his ear," Aunt Marty corrected her. "And it wasn't for a woman. In a psychotic episode, van Gogh lunged at his friend—the painter Paul Gauguin—with a razor. He didn't cut him, but later that night, wracked with guilt, he sliced a chunk out of his own ear."

Mom gave her sister a look. I looked at her, too—with awe. That day, I saw how much there was to know in the world. How much more lay beyond Odessa.

The three of us walked more than I've ever walked in my life. My aunt paid for everything—even my sparkly Barney's sandals that were ridiculously expensive and so cool I couldn't wait to show Celeste.

"When you're in my town," Aunt Marty said, "you're my guest."

I loved every part of the city—the smell of kebabs grilling in the sidewalk food stands, the blasts of heat from the subway grates, the buzz in the air, the clicking of expensive shoes. Eventually, Mom chilled out, though she steadfastly refused to cross the street against a red light no matter what everyone else did.

"These crazy bicycle messengers don't care *what* color the streetlight is!"

That night, as exhausted as I was exhilarated, I met Aunt Marty's handsome husband for the first time, too. Uncle Richard. He was a divorce lawyer who wore a silver suit and smelled like cologne. His hands were tan, and his gold wedding band looked like he polished it every day. When I saw the way my uncle gazed at my aunt, I knew how a man should view a woman. His eyes sparkled with lust, love, and awe. He looked as though he'd never fully understand his wife, but that was okay. Even at eleven years old, I knew I wanted a man to look at me like that one day.

Uncle Richard joined the three of us for a late dinner on the sky-high balcony of their apartment overlooking the East River. After dark, we popped popcorn and watched fireworks explode over the river. Just like a real family.

"What do you think of our little town?" Uncle Richard asked me.

"I want to live here," I said.

"You don't mean that, Ruthie," Mom said. She coughed and cleared her throat.

"Yes. Yes, I do."

Mom coughed again. "Does anyone know what's holding this balcony up?"

• • •

The thing I loved most about New York—besides my aunt Marty—was the lack of time obsession. Nobody ate lunch at noon, dinner at six. They didn't need to get to the drugstore before it closed at seven. New Yorkers were *free*. Nobody noticed what you ordered on your pizza or bought at the supermarket or wore when you didn't have anything that wasn't in the laundry. They didn't ask where you lived in Middletown, then frown when you told them you lived in Odessa. They didn't care that your house needed paint and you didn't have a dad to do it.

"Ms. Bayer, may I show you to your room?"

Renata, the housekeeper, stood at the sliding glass door leading to the balcony. She must have responded to some private signal, because Aunt Marty nodded and said, "Good night, sweetheart. Uncle Richard and I need to talk to your mom."

Mom looked a little wild-eyed, but that could have been her balcony fear. I noticed she was clutching the edge of the drapes.

"This was the best day of my whole life," I said, nearly bursting into tears. Kissing everyone good night, I followed Renata to a bedroom at the far end of the giant apartment.

The guest room was all white, too. With a huge window seat in a soft, robelike fabric. The bed was enormous—a giant marshmallow—and the sheets were so smooth I was sure they'd been ironed. Everything smelled clean and new. The bathroom looked like fancy hotel bathrooms I'd seen on TV. There were gold knobs on the sink and tub, fluffy white towels that were bigger than I was, wrapped bars of soap. Best of all, Mom had her own room. This was my private space for the entire weekend.

Renata said, "Your clothes are unpacked and in the drawers. I've left bottled water on the bedside table in case you get thirsty."

Water? Unpacking? Was this the life, or what?!

"If you want to watch a movie, press the blue button."

Renata picked up a remote control and pressed a blue button. A frosted cabinet across from the bed opened, revealing a huge television and rows and rows of DVDs.

"Do you have cable?" I asked, excited.

"They have everything," said Renata. "But only G-rated, okay?"

"Of course," I said, grinning.

Renata said good night, then left me alone. I'd never felt more grown-up in my life.

After brushing my teeth and washing my face, I crawled into the yummy bed. My head sank into the pillow. I felt like I was floating. I could have fallen asleep instantly, but no way was I going to sleep in New York City! Not when I had cable and any movie I wanted to watch all on my own.

As I scanned the video library, I saw a stack of glossy

magazines on the shiny glass nightstand. *Fabrique*—the fashion magazine that weighs a ton and smells like a department store. The models on the cover wear skirts up to *here* and necklines down to *there*. Their hair is always full and puffy and blown by a fan.

Of course, I had to pick it up. Mom never let me read this kind of commercial "trash." Inside, sprinkled among ads for sunglasses and wrinkle cream and purses that cost a thousand bucks, were articles about getting yours and giving hell and burning calories through Tantric sex. Whatever *that* was. Mom would freak out if she knew I was reading it! Of course, I studied every page.

Suddenly, my eyes bugged out of my head.

I blinked. I stared. It couldn't be.

There, in *Fabrique*, lying on a white couch, in a white suit, with a red feathery thing around her neck, was my aunt Marty.

I blinked again. Yes, it was her.

The photograph was small. It wasn't a fashion shot. Aunt Marty, with a sly look in her eye, was staring at me from the top of an article called, "Martine on Men."

"A group of guys is like a pack of male dogs in the park," I read. "They sniff each other out, snarl at the weakest pup, hang with dogs about their size and age. If left to their own devices, they'll find some silly reason to work themselves into a frenzy and rumble. It's all about strutting their stuff in front of other males, about not showing weakness. Follow a male dog home, however, and you'll see him curl up in his mistress's lap, tongue hanging out, begging her to tickle his tummy in that special spot that makes his leg go nuts."

Grabbing another issue of *Fabrique*, I checked the table of contents and found the same thing: "Martine on Men." Beneath the title, the caption read, "Musings from New York's Goddess of Love."

My *aunt* was New York's Goddess of *Love*?!

"Few things are more attractive to a man than a woman who couldn't care less about him," Aunt Marty wrote in her column.

"You want him to be interested in you?" she wrote in another. "Lead an interesting life."

I couldn't believe it! Then, I *could*. Of course my aunt was a Goddess of Love! It was obvious. Why wouldn't she write a column about men? She knew everything! Even as a kid, I knew I'd stumbled on to the key that would unlock my pathetic life.

"Oh my *God*," I said out loud. My aunt, my only living relative, is an *expert* on the one thing I'll never know anything about: the male species. How could I know about boys when my mother is practically a *nun* and my only male role model—Mr. Arthur—has curled toes, hairy ears, and a mind full of useless trivia?

Though I tried to stay awake, I fell asleep reading one of

her columns. That night, I dreamed I was standing at the edge of a bright blue pool of water. I wore a flowing white dress. The sun lit my red hair. After I dipped one perfectly polished (crimson!) toe in the water, a man rushed out to dry my foot. Then he kissed it. I smiled, knowing this was just another ho-hum day for a Goddess in paradise.

Asleep in that cloud of a bed, everything changed. That weekend, I realized my aunt Marty was the woman I wanted to grow up to be. Finally, I had someone who could teach me about *life. How lucky,* I thought, *can a know-nothing kid from Delaware get?*

"WE CAME ALL THIS WAY FOR A *DAY?*"

I was furious.

"It wasn't a vacation, Ruthie," Mom said, zipping up my suitcase while I still lay in bed under the fluffy cloud comforter in the guest room. "Martha and Richard wanted to talk to me. Which they did last night. Now it's time to go home."

"I don't want to go home."

"Tough cookies," Mom said.

I sat up. The imprint of the down pillow was still on my cheek. "Just because you talked to them doesn't mean we have to leave!"

"Where are those expensive sandals?" Mom asked. "I want you to give them back."

"*What?!*"

"You're *my* daughter. I won't have anyone buying your love."

Mom was on her knees now, looking under the bed. My new sandals were in the bathroom where I'd worn them last night so I could hear the *tap, tap* of real leather soles on the tile floor. How, I wondered, could I make it into the bathroom without my mother seeing? Could I hide those sandals in my underpants?

"Get up, Ruthie. We're leaving in ten minutes."

"But, Mom," I whined, "I love it here. Can't we stay one more night? Please. Can't we?"

"No."

"Pleeeeease?"

"*No.*"

I tried one more avenue. "You'll never believe what I found out last night. About Aunt Marty. She's *famous*. Did you know that? She's in a magazine and everything!"

Mom froze. I could literally see the blood draining from her face.

"Who told you?" my mother asked through her teeth.

"Nobody told me. I read it!" Reaching under the covers, I pulled out one of the heavy issues of *Fabrique*.

"Where did you get that?" Mom snatched it from my hand.

"Right here. On the table."

"In your *room*?"

"It's just a magazine."

I thought her head would explode.

"Martha knows I don't want you reading this garbage," she said, flinging back the covers to reveal several issues of *Fabrique*. The flowery smell of the perfume samples rose up in the air. Mom gasped. I felt like I'd been caught with drugs.

"I want you dressed and at the elevator in five minutes."

My mother stormed out of the room. I leaped up, ran into the bathroom, and grabbed my sparkly sandals. Wrapping them in my pajamas, I stuffed them in the deepest part of my overnight bag, hoping my mother would never again look at my feet.

Uncle Richard had already left for work. Three places were set at the breakfast table. A pot of coffee was brewing in the kitchen. Fresh orange juice was poured into tiny glasses. I smelled hot muffins.

"Stay for breakfast at least," Aunt Marty said, her eyes puffy and red.

"I'm sorry, Martha, we can't," Mom said.

"Yes we can!" I protested.

"No," Mom said, her face so set it looked like it was carved out of a block of wood, "we can't."

I couldn't decide whether to cry or scream. So I just stood there, in my aunt's gorgeous dining room, a simmering volcano.

Grabbing my suitcase, Mom made a beeline for the elevator and pressed the button a thousand times. Aunt Marty made a beeline for me.

"We'll have to see each other another time," she said gently, taking both of my hands in hers.

"It's not fair," I said.

She sighed. "It is what it is."

With that, my aunt led me to the elevator. The doors opened the moment we got there. A doorman was inside. He took my suitcase and held the doors open for my mother and me.

"Thank you, Martha," Mom said coolly, stepping inside.

I tried to say "thank you," too, but the words were all choked in my throat. So I threw my arms around my aunt and hugged her tight, as if everything I wanted to say could be squeezed into her.

"C'mon, Ruthie," Mom said, as she yanked me into the elevator.

The last thing I saw were Aunt Marty's teary eyes and the bright sunlight behind her, shining like a halo.

The car ride back to Odessa felt like it lasted a *week*. I refused to speak a single word. My jaw throbbed from being shut so tightly. Finally, as we crossed the Delaware Bridge, I couldn't hold it in any longer.

"Why?" I demanded.

"Why what?" Mom said.

"Why did we have to leave? Why won't you let Aunt Marty be my aunt?"

Mom sighed. "She *is* your aunt."

"What happened last night? Why don't we ever visit New York? Why doesn't Aunt Marty ever visit us?"

My mother's eyes looked weary. She seemed to shrink behind the steering wheel. "When you're old enough to hear the truth, I'll tell you."

My eyes bugged out of my head. "I'm *eleven*!"

"You're not ready," Mom said.

"Yes, I am."

"No, you're not."

"Yes. I. Am." Arms crossed, I was prepared to go on all day.

Mom put her blinker on. There was a rest stop off the turnpike ahead. She pulled over, turned the ignition off, and faced me.

"I'm only going to say this once, Ruthie," she said. "I have a very good reason for keeping you away from my sister. One day, I'll tell you what it is. And *I* will decide when the timing is right. Not you. I don't want to hear about Martha or Richard or New York or *Fabrique*. You are forbidden to call or write them. Do you understand me?"

"But, Mom, I—"

"Do you understand me?"

I knew that stony look. Mount *Mom*more. There was no budging her.

"I mean it, Ruthie. My sister is dead to me."

"Why does she have to be dead to *me*?"

Mom started the car and pulled back onto the highway. "Because that's the way it is," she said. Then she refused to say anything more. For the rest of the way, my mother stared out the windshield, her fists tight on the steering wheel.

I never mentioned my aunt Marty again. Not to my mother, anyway. But I read *Fabrique* every month in the Middletown Wawa near school. Mr. Shabala, the owner, keeps saying, "This isn't a library!" but he doesn't kick me out because he knows I'll just go to the Pathmark down the street.

Celeste, Frankie, and I also dream of turning eighteen and taking a train to New York and eating sushi on Aunt Marty's balcony. We plan to stay up all night so we can see for ourselves what the city looks like when everyone really is asleep.

Far back in the corner of my closet, I still have my sparkly sandals. Secretly, I wore them until my toes hung so far over the front that they looked ridiculous. They are, by far, my favorite possession.

If Mom thought she could control my *mind*, she was totally mistaken. Aunt Marty may be dead to her, but she's alive and perfect in my heart. In the three years since I've seen her, my aunt—New York's Goddess of Love—has become a Goddess to me, too. If my mother thought I would stop thinking about Aunt Marty, stop wanting to *be* her, she was as wrong as she was to think I'd stay in Odessa all my life.

"AUNT MARTY?"

"Ruthie?"

The phone trembles in my hand. I'm sure she can hear the blood pumping through my veins. Mom is downstairs.

"Yes," I say, my voice squeaky. "It's me."

"Ruthie!" Aunt Marty's voice sounds exactly the way I

remember it. Like the soft, warm comforter on her guest bed.

"Has something happened to your mother?" she asks, alarmed.

"No, no. She's fine. Well, she's crazy, but that's normal." My aunt's laughter tickles my ears like tiny feathers.

I'm finding it hard to breathe. I keep looking at the door, listening for footsteps. I've taken the pillow off my head, but I keep it close. If necessary, I'll shove the phone into the pillowcase. Or, I'll start calling Aunt Marty "Celeste" and explain later.

"Are you okay?" Aunt Marty asks.

I swallow. "No."

I hear the air leave my aunt's body. "Oh, honey. What's wrong?"

"I . . . I . . ."

"Are you hurt?"

"No . . . I'm—it's just—"

"Whatever it is, you can tell me. I'll help you."

Pressing my eyes closed, I take a deep breath. My throat is tight. My heart is thudding. My mouth is dry. I can't get the words out, but I have to. It's an emergency.

"Oh, Aunt Marty," I finally spit out, bursting into tears. "I'm in *love*!"

IT'S SATURDAY. THE DAY OF MY DOOM. I COULDN'T SLEEP
at all last night, and my hair looks it. It's a mass of knots on
one side. And the red squiggly lines in my eyeballs look like
I've been crying, but I haven't. I've been lying awake, listening to my heart thud, wondering how Mom is going to kill
me.

   It happened so fast. One minute I was on the phone

asking Aunt Marty for advice about revving up my girl power and snagging Perry Gould before Perfect Girl got her claws into him. The next minute Aunt Marty said, "I'll be there this weekend."

"Here?" I gulped.

"It's time to end this nonsense," she said.

"Nonsense?" I suddenly lost the ability to say anything original.

"Your mother can't keep me away from you forever. Don't tell her, Ruthie. It'll be our little surprise."

"She hates surprises."

"We'll have a nice talk, you and me."

"Hey, I know! E-mail!"

"Nonsense. I'll see you in Odessa on Saturday."

So, it's Saturday morning, and I'm yanking a brush through my tangled hair. I hear Mom and Mr. Arthur downstairs in the kitchen. I smell bacon. I feel like throwing up.

Number One: I have nothing to wear. Green Costco capri pants and brown Payless sandals? What was I thinking? Don't I own *anything* black? Can I cram my feet into my old Barney's sandals? Tossing my hairbrush onto my bed, I frantically flip through my closet.

"Ruthie!"

Mom calls from downstairs. My heart stops.

"Bacon or sausage?" she yells.

How can I possibly think about pork when Aunt Marty

is moments away?!

"Do we have any *turkey* bacon?" I call down the stairs. Best to act normal, I decide. Mom will be suspicious otherwise.

"No," Mom says. "I'm making you sausage."

"Okay!" I call out, my voice chirpy. "I'll be down in a few minutes!"

In desperation, I pull off my capris and pull on old Levi's and a new T-shirt. No shoes at all.

Number Two: The whole town will know that Aunt Marty has arrived. It's impossible to keep *any* secrets in this town, much less a big one, like New York's Goddess of Love coming home. And how long before the *reason* for her visit is revealed? To personally counsel her virginal niece on seducing the boy next door.

Yes, I'm definitely going to throw up.

"Your orange juice is on the table, Ruthie," Mom shouts.

That's when I hear it. A car pulling up. My heart plummets to the pit of my stomach. My upper lip sprouts sweat. Leaping for the window, I peel back the curtain and peer out.

There she is.

Her shiny gold car sparkles in the morning sunlight. She pokes one pointy toe of her strappy red high heels out the car door. Then the other. Rising up, she inhales the warm air. She stretches like a pampered Persian cat. I watch her run both hands down the front of her narrow rose-colored skirt, adjust her big black sunglasses, lift a tan leather suitcase out of the trunk, and smooth her white-blond hair.

I witness all of it from the window of my messy beige room.

It's still true. My aunt Marty is a *Goddess*.

Diving for my bedroom door, I fly down the stairs and race into the living room just as Aunt Marty knocks on the door.

"I'll get it!" I screech.

Practically pulling the doorknob off, I fling open the door.

"You're here," I say, breathless.

Aunt Marty smiles and floats through the front door, dropping her soft leather suitcase on the hardwood floor.

"Beautiful, sweet Ruthie," she says, her eyes peering into mine. "I had no idea you'd be so grown-up. How old are you now? Sixteen? Seventeen?"

"Fourteen." I beam.

"Let me look at you."

Holding one shoulder in each hand, my aunt scans me up and down.

"My goodness," she coos. "Fourteen and so mature already. Such a lovely young woman."

I glow. You can always count on Levi's.

Aunt Marty reaches her hand to my face and gently cups my chin. Even after a three-hour drive from New York

City to Odessa—the time it's *supposed* to take when you're not terrified that a deranged insect will fly in the window—she looks like she just stepped out of a salon. She smells heavenly, too. Her breath is sweet, like she uses expensive custom-made mouthwash. *Natural* mouthwash, each jade-green peppermint leaf squeezed just for her. Tipping my head up she says, "Your eyes are stunning, Ruthie. That's the deepest blue I've ever seen."

A giggle escapes my throat like a dainty cough.

"And your red hair . . . do you have any idea how much women pay to reproduce that color?"

My eyelashes flutter. I'm not kidding, they *flutter.*

"It's been much too long." Aunt Marty takes me into her arms and holds me close. I melt into the soft fabric of her white linen shirt. I shut my eyes and imagine passing straight through her body, implanting her soul into mine on the way out.

"The grease on your sausages is con*geal*ing," Mom calls from the kitchen. "Who's at the door?"

I hear the scuffle of my mother's footsteps. *Oh God, she's wearing her inside shoes.*

"Here we go," Aunt Marty says, pulling away from me. "Brace yourself for Hurricane Fay."

Mortified, I see that my mother is still in her bathrobe. The ugly plaid one she's had for a gazillion years.

"Look who dropped by," I say, my voice barely audible.

"Hello, Fay," Aunt Marty says.

Mom is speechless. Her hair is a knotted ball of wool.

"I've come for a visit," Aunt Marty says, confidently walking up to my mother and hugging her. Mom doesn't move. She doesn't say a word. I'd prefer a hurricane. Anything but the disheveled mannequin frozen in the center of the room.

Side by side, my mom and her older sister are the "before" and "after" of an extreme makeover show. I can barely look.

"Your breakfast is in the kitchen, Ruthie." Mom suddenly breaks her silence.

"I'm not hungry," I say.

Her teeth press together. "Lemonade, Martha?"

Creasing my eyebrows, I think, *Lemonade?*

"Lemonade would be marvelous!" Aunt Marty claps her satiny hands together. Her diamond wedding ring flashes in the sunlight. I notice her red nail polish doesn't have a single chip. "It must be nearly ninety degrees outside. I bought an iced cappuccino in the city before I left, but I'm absolutely dying of thirst right now. I can't imagine anything more refreshing than a lemonade. What a gracious suggestion, Fay. Ruthie, will you have one, too?"

"I'd adore a lemonade!"

Mom gives me a weird look. I know what she's thinking. *Adore?* I can't believe it, either.

"Ruthie and I will get it, Martha. Have a seat. We'll be right back."

Mom marches for the kitchen and shoots me a look that lets me know I'd better follow her . . . or *else*. I scurry behind, my bare feet slapping the floor. Mr. Arthur is sitting at the kitchen table, reading the newspaper and eating oatmeal.

"Hello, girls," he says.

"Since when do we have lemonade?!" I ask my mother, racing for the refrigerator door.

Mom slams it shut the moment I open it.

"Of course we don't have lemonade!" she snaps, her voice dangerously close to needing an exorcism. "What is *she* doing here?"

"I . . . I . . . I have no idea," I lie.

"Did you call her?"

"Call her? Why would you ask me that?"

"Did you?" Mom's red face is scaring me.

I get all indignant. "God, Mom," I say, "don't you trust me? How was I supposed to know who was at the door?"

Wriggling away from the refrigerator and my mother's demonic stare, I grab three glasses from the cupboard. "We'll have to have water now, since you *lied* about the lemonade."

My mother's eyes look wild. She says, "I'm not leaving this kitchen until you make me a promise."

"Did you at least refill the ice cube trays?" Flying across the kitchen, I fling open the freezer door and groan. "Mom! There are only three half cubes!"

She slams the freezer door shut in my face. "Promise," she hisses.

"Promise what?"

"Promise first."

"How can I promise if I don't know what you wan—"

"PROMISE!"

I stare.

"Everything okay in there?" Aunt Marty calls from the living room.

"We'll be right out," Mom calls back, her voice unnaturally high. Then, her face gets twisted and she mouths the word, "Promise."

Any moment, I expect my mother's head to spin completely around and pea soup to hurl from her mouth.

"*Okay*," I spit out. "I *promise*. What is it?"

My mother presses her mouth right up to my ear and whispers, "Promise me you'll say no."

"To what?"

"Just promise."

"Mom!"

"My sister is a black widow spider, Ruthie. Once someone is caught in her web, there's no getting out."

I roll my eyes. "She thinks I look seventeen, Mom. She's awesome."

Mom squeezes my arm. "I'm not letting you go until you promise."

"Owww . . ."

"Promise."

The squeeze gets tighter. "I'm pretty sure this is child abuse," I say, trying to free my arm.

"I mean it, Ruthie."

Jerking free, I say, "All *right*! If you're going to go insane over it, I promise to say no to whatever she's going to ask me. Man! She's my only relative. Thanks a lot, Mother."

"Don't mention it," Mom says, releasing me. "Now, help me get her out of here before she unpacks."

WE'RE TOO LATE. BY THE TIME I BRING THREE GLASSES of iceless tap water into the living room, Aunt Marty has already draped a lavender silk shawl over the barf-colored afghan on the back of our couch and removed Mom's funky window treatments.

"Don't worry," she says, when she notices Mom's alarmed expression, "I'll have new curtains up before the painters are finished."

"What painters?"

"You don't actually *like* this color, do you, Fay?"

Mom clamps her teeth together.

"I don't know how long I'll be staying," Aunt Marty says. "Why not make it beautiful?"

"What do you mean, you don't know how long you're staying?"

Still holding the water tray, I watch the two of them like a spectator at a tennis match.

"Don't worry," says Aunt Marty, "I'll make myself useful."

"By changing everything?" My mother's nostrils flare.

"Let's get Ruthie's opinion."

A jolt of electricity shoots through my arms.

"Would you like to see a little color on the walls?" Aunt Marty asks.

I freeze. Is this the question Mom is worried about? *Paint?*

"No," I say. Hey, a promise is a promise.

"I'm sure you'll change your mind when you see it done."

Aunt Marty completely disregards both me and my mom. Wow. How do you get confidence like that? Was she born with it? Is there hope for someone whose mother knits baby blankies for a living?

Old Mr. Arthur waddles into the living room.

"We have company!" he exclaims.

"This is my sister, Martha," Mom says icily.

Aunt Marty reaches her arms out to greet Mr. Arthur and, I swear, he looks at her boobs and blushes. He extends one speckled hand and says, *"Enchanté."*

"Call me Marty," Aunty Marty says, ignoring the handshake and hugging him. "We're practically family."

Mr. Arthur just grins. I can tell he hasn't heard a word.

"You can't barge in here and disrupt our lives, Martha," Mom shouts. Then she stomps out of the room . . . except, in her slippers, it's more like messy scuffling. Me, I can only think of one thing to say.

"Water?"

Mr. Arthur seems to hear me because he says, "Don't mind if I do." Bizarrely, he takes the whole tray from me and shuffles after my mother into the kitchen. Really, the two of them are made for each other.

Aunt Marty looks at me and shrugs. "I wasn't really thirsty."

I laugh. My aunt enfolds me in her arms and says, "Now sit next to your auntie and tell her all about Perry and this perfect girl who thinks she stands a chance."

"OKAY," I SAY TO AUNT MARTY. "HERE'S THE THING."

And it all comes tumbling out.

First, I explain, falling in love with Perry Gould was *so* not in my plans. I'd imagined my first love to be someone from somewhere *else*. He would bump into me at Dover Mall. *Literally.* I'd be walking with Celeste and Frankie, giggling (make that laughing luxuriously with my head tilted back). He'd round a corner, wearing dark glasses indoors, and we would collide.

"S'cuse me," the boy would mutter, and keep walking. But a few steps later, I'd turn around and see that he'd turned around, too. He'd be watching me, his sunglasses low on his nose. I'd slightly raise one eyebrow and keep going.

At the food court, in the Ranch One line, he would suddenly appear behind us. We'd wordlessly connect (who needs words when you have *electricity*?). Secretly, I'd feel glad he chose me over Celeste. For once, there'd be a cute guy who doesn't even notice her. (He won't be mean or anything; he'll just only have eyes for *me*.) As for Frankie, well, she's never admitted to liking *any* boy yet. Her fantasies revolve more around fat-free ice cream.

Celeste would feel happy for me, but slightly jealous. Which *can* be done. I've felt both happy for—and jealous of—Celeste Serrano ever since we were in sixth grade, when she sat next to me in the cafeteria and asked, "How can you *read* while you *eat*?" I was stunned that this exotic Latina with long black hair, black eyes, and perfectly smooth, chocolate skin would sit next to freckly me.

I'm not a nerd or anything. My red hair is unusual, which I like. When it's not all frizzed out. My boobs are still nonexistent, but the rest of my body is okay. Except for my freckles, which make me crazy. They pop out all over the place when I, like, pass a *window*. I wear sunscreen all the time, but it just makes my face look greasy *and* freckly. And my white skin blushes fast. All a teacher has to do is say my name in class and I instantly blush and sweat. Mom says the blushing will stop eventually. But, she sighs, "Sweating is forever."

God, I hope she's wrong.

The truth is, ever since I met New York's Goddess of Love, I decided to view myself as a Goddess in the making—with the unfortunate exception of being clueless when it comes to enticing boys. Admittedly a stumbling block on my way to Goddesshood. Still, I'm definitely pretty enough to be Perry Gould's girlfriend. *If* I could get him to stop treating me as his childhood pal!

I sigh. Like I do every time I think of how far I am from Perfect Girl.

"How could this happen?" I ask Aunt Marty in our living room. "Perfect Girl appears the moment I fall in love?"

She asks, "You're sure Perry is interested in her?"

My shoulders sag. "I'm not sure of anything anymore."

I flash on my food court fantasy. In it, Perfect *Boy* is definitely not Perry Gould. My Perfect Boy would saunter over to my table. I'd dip a french fry into barbecue sauce, and he'd lean down close to my ear and say, "There's this party in Dover."

I'd say, "Oh yeah?"

He'd ask, "Wanna go?"

I'd say, "Sure," without worrying about my mom going all mental or wondering how I'd get there, or how I'd get home. Then he'd ask, "Where can I pick you up?" and I'd know he was not only a gentleman, but sixteen, too.

Just looking at him would turn my insides into Cream of Wheat.

Of course, my vision is so far from reality it might as well be on Mars. Mom won't even let me go to Dover *Mall* without her. So, a party? With a boy? In a car? Yeah right, I'd have better luck convincing my mother to pierce her own navel. ("It'll look cool! All the mothers are doing it!")

Then again, I'm living proof that the weirdest stuff *can* happen. Like the fact that I'm now feeling all Cream of Wheat over Perry Gould.

"I need major help," I tell my aunt. "And I don't have much time."

She hugs me tight and says, "Don't worry. I'm here. Perry Gould will soon be crawling at your feet."

She looks down at my bare toes.

"First stop," she says, "a pedicure."

AT SCHOOL, CELESTE AND FRANKIE ARE BUZZING ABOUT IT.

"New York's Goddess of Love is in *Odessa*?"

"Does she have, like, a different lover for every day of the week?"

"Is she nice, or bitchy?"

At first, I feel all superior. "She's nice," I say. "We're tight."

I wiggle my freshly painted toenails and giggle over retelling the awesome time we had at Tip-Top Nails in Middletown over the weekend. (The truth: Mom came with us and totally ruined everything by refusing a pedicure for herself and insisting I wear only "natural-looking" polish. "Red," she said, "is for hookers." Aunt Marty wears red polish and looks like a *Goddess*.)

"Her husband is a major New York attorney," I say. "They're an awesome couple."

By the end of the school day, as I make my way to the bus, a new feeling melts over me.

"She's a really private person," I say sullenly. "She hates when people talk about her."

I doubt that's true, not that I know. The fact is, I barely know anything at all about my aunt. Which bums me out. My friends are all curious, but I don't have answers. Not that it stops them from pounding me with questions.

"Is she as beautiful as her picture in *Fabrique*?"

"Is she worldly? Sexy?"

"Does she look like she can turn men into quivering masses of adoring goo?"

"When can we come over and meet her?"

Finally, I say to Frankie, "Did you eat garlic for lunch?"

Her hand flies up to her mouth.

"I have bad breath?" she asks through her fingers.

"Let's just say you're safe from vampires."

Celeste breathes on me and asks, "How's mine?"

I say, "A little gum wouldn't hurt."

While my friends fish through their packs for gum, I swallow my guilt and wonder why I'm acting so bitchy. Then, it hits me. After fourteen years of being the daughter of the sperm donor, the sister of no one, the roommate of Mr. Arthur—I'm now Ruthie Bayer, niece of Martine on Men. She's *mine*. I thought I wanted to share her. But I don't.

"Hey." Perry nods his head as he passes by us.

Instantly, I flush. "Hey!" I reply. Though I try to sound casual, "Hey" flies out of my mouth with an exclamation point. I'm such a spaz.

"Hey, Jen," I hear Perry say behind me.

My head spins around. Jenna Wilson emerges from a crowd of kids like a blooming rosebud. She wears pink from head to toe. Her flip-flops are even decorated with fuchsia feathers. God, she's so . . . so . . . *girly.* Looking at my brown sandals, I feel like a truck driver. Even with my fresh pedi.

"Hey, Perry," Perfect Girl says, with the perfect amount of friendliness, calm, and dignity. She smiles. Her cheeks are perfectly pink! My heart hits the floor.

Perry's abbreviation of Jenna's name feels like a stab wound. Since when does he call her "Jen"? Since when does he call her *anything*? And how does she know his name?

"Cute shorts," Jenna says to me as she walks past. Glancing down at my denim shorts from Target, I can't tell if she's making fun of me or not.

"Thanks," I say, calling after her. "My aunt Martine bought them for me in New York."

Celeste and Frankie both roll their eyes. They were with me in Target last month when the shorts were on sale.

"I thought Martine was a private person," Celeste says.

"Yeah," Frankie says, "I thought she hates when people talk about her."

What can I say? My emotions are on tilt.

"There's my bus," I blurt out, turning my back on my two friends and racing for the bus ride home with Perry.

WE SIT NEAR THE BACK OF THE BUS . . . OUR NORMAL SPOT.
My heart is bursting out of my chest. This whole "Jen" thing
is freaking me out. Do they have a class together? One that
I'm not in? Did she *sit* next to him? Did he get up and move
so he could sit next to her?

I can barely breathe.

Thank God Aunt Marty is here.

But—and this is a humongous but—after our pedicures over the weekend, Mom treated Aunt Marty like she was a serial killer or something. She never left us alone for a moment. Which totally sucks since there's no way I'm going to tell my mother that I need time alone with her sister so she can help me snag a guy. Already, last night's dinner was so tense it nearly snapped.

"You don't like my baked chicken?" Mom asked, her lips tight.

"It's tasty enough," Aunt Marty replied. "I just prefer to use meat as a *spice*. A touch to jazz up my vegetables."

"You're not eating your creamed corn, either."

"I'm not that hungry."

"What about the mashed potatoes?"

"I try not to overload on carbs."

Mom scoffed. "Are you calling me fat?"

"Of course not," said Aunt Marty. "It's just that corn is really more of a bread than a vegetable."

"Is that what they say in New York? Out here, corn-*bread* is a bread."

Mom's lips were now pressed so tightly together her mouth was a hyphen at the bottom of her face.

"Bet you didn't know that Delaware was once filled with five million peach trees," Mr. Arthur piped up, oblivious as usual.

"I do remember something about that," Aunt Marty said, smiling warmly at him. Then she turned to Mom and said, "I'd love to do the cooking while I'm here, Fay. Do you have a stove-top grill?"

Mom's nostrils opened and closed like an angry bull's. "We like plain food. Don't we, Ruthie?"

I gulped. What could I say? Aunt Marty was right. The chicken was tasty *enough*. If you liked chewing rubber bands. And creamed corn was a lot like eating oatmeal. I'd been bugging my mom to buy a George Foreman grill, but all she'd said was, "What does a boxer know about cooking?"

"Ruthie?"

"My room is your old room, right, Aunt Marty?" I quickly changed the subject.

"Ah, yes," she said. "My years in solitary confinement."

Over-laughing, I ignored the maternal glare boring into the side of my head and asked, "How is Uncle Richard?"

Aunt Marty inhaled extravagantly. "What can I say? Richard is exactly like *Richard*."

I exploded in giggles, though it wasn't that funny. I tossed my head back and enhanced my real laugh with a fake howl.

"It's not like we can afford a private chef!" Mom banged her fist on the table. The water in my glass leaped up in a little wave. I swallowed my phony laugh with an embarrassing, burplike gulp.

"Georgia stole all our thunder as the Peach State," Mr. Arthur said. "How do you like them apples?"

Aunt Marty genuinely laughed. Before my eyes, Mr.

Arthur turned into a puppy. I kept waiting for him to curl up on Aunt Marty's lap, roll over, and beg her to tickle his tummy in that spot that makes his leg go nuts.

"So," I say to Perry, as the bus rumbles toward Odessa, "I'm here for you if you ever want to talk."

Frantically scanning my memory for Aunt Marty's advice in *Fabrique*, I remember that she once wrote, "It's not that guys don't talk, girls don't *listen*."

Perry looks at me and says, "Thanks."

"And, um, it doesn't bother me that you like astronomy," I say, remembering something about accepting guys for who they *are*, not who you want them to be.

Perry glares. "Gee, that's mighty generous of you, Ruthie."

"I mean, if you ever feel like you want to cry, that would be okay with me."

"Cry?"

"You know, uh, if you feel like being *emotional*. Other girls lie about it, but not me. I can handle tears. I can cope with deep feelings."

Perry blinks. "Ruthie, you are seriously warped."

"What I'm saying is—"

"Define *photosphere*."

"Huh?"

Looking down, I notice Perry has pulled his iQuest handheld computer out of his baggy pants pocket. He pops in the Science Quiz cartridge.

"I'll give you a hint," he says. "The sun has a visible photosphere."

I roll my eyes. Then I stop myself. Isn't this exactly what "Martine on Men" was talking about? Accepting a guy for who he really is?

"The yellow part?" I ask.

"Sort of. The photosphere of a star is the atmosphere of electromagnetic gases and stellar winds."

Perry goes on. "Name the star nearest to our solar system."

"Reese Witherspoon?"

He doesn't laugh. "Proxima Centauri, a triple star about twenty-five trillion miles from Earth."

See why Celeste thinks Perry walks the Earth with a blinding nerd-aura glowing all around him?

"Doesn't sound very 'proxima' to me." That's all *I* can think of to say. Which is cool because I end up sitting back, leaning my head against the seat, and letting Perry be Perry for the rest of the ride.

IF AUNT MARTY WEREN'T SMACK IN THE CENTER OF THE
room, blowing wisps of blond hair from her mouth, I would
have backed out and checked the address. When I get
home, my "home" is gone. Our on-sale, flea market, home-
sewn, found-on-the-curb-on-garbage-day furniture is gone.
Vanished without a trace. The walls are the most beautiful
blue I've ever seen. Two white wicker couches sit opposite

one another in the center of the room. Throw pillows, in antique flag fabric, add color; a quilt made from embroidered handkerchiefs is draped over the back. Mr. Arthur's burled coffee table (that was once used as an ashtray, judging by the burn marks) has been replaced by a hand-painted pine chest. The formerly dust-bunnied wood floor is covered with a huge braided rug in different shades of yellow. Mom's mismatched curtains are gone. Window *treatments*, in a Ralph Lauren-ish floral, complement the overstuffed striped cushions of the new white rocking chairs. Our crummy old house in Odessa is now a magazine cover.

"It's . . . it's . . ." I'm speechless.

"Just a few pieces from my house in the Hamptons," Aunt Marty says. "They arrived an hour ago. I figure, why not surround ourselves with lovely things? The painters are finishing up the sunporch."

"Are we allowed to sit in here?"

She laughs. "Of course! The true sign of being a grown-up is having a white couch. We're grown-ups, aren't we?"

Isn't that *so* like a Goddess?

"How did this happen so fast?" I ask.

My aunt puts both hands on my shoulders. "Once you decide to do something, it doesn't take long to get it done. Most people waste all their time deciding."

That reminds me. "Where's Mom?"

"In the garden, I think," Aunt Marty says, knocking on

the wall that separates the living room from the dining room. "Do you think this is weight-bearing?"

Is *this* the question Mom warned me about?

"No," I answer, still true to my word.

"Good. This old house could use a real face-lift."

Mom *is* in the garden. Which isn't a good sign. Her garden is where she retreats when she's upset. When Taylor's Diner went belly-up and she lost her waitressing job, she planted a whole row of hyacinths and pulled out the calendulas. When Mr. Arthur was in the hospital having the eye surgery that caused him to wear his Coke-bottle glasses, she pruned the redbud tree so much it looked like bamboo. When she was denied admission to Odessa's Homeowner's Association on what she called a "technicality," she planted a row of yellow Towne and Country rosebushes to block out her view of the street. Now, I find her sitting on the stone bench she's placed in the center of the herb section, yanking sweet basil out by the roots.

"Are you okay?" I ask.

She doesn't answer me. A sharp green smell fills the air.

"How can you sit here when the walls of your house are coming down?"

My mother slumps her shoulders. "She's knocking down walls?"

"I think so," I say. Then I wait for an explosion, an

explanation, *something*. But Mom is now furiously pinching back the cilantro. Finally, I wave my hands in front of her face. "Yoo-hoo, Mother. Remember me? The redhead who lives with you?"

Mom brushes a clump of dirt off her lap, looks up at me. "Sit down, honey." She pats the stone bench. "It's time."

"Time for what?"

"You're old enough to hear the truth."

My stomach lurches. The *truth*? This is it? The moment of truth I've been waiting for all my life? Out here in the garden, I'm finally going to hear why I, too, have been kept in solitary confinement?

Dazed, I lower my butt to the bench.

Instantly, my armpits feel wet. Images of "the truth" race through my mind. My mother was once a man. Unable to bear another minute being trapped inside a hairy chest, she undergoes sex-change surgery and goes from Frank to Fay.

No, that can't be it. No way would a woman trapped in a man's body emerge with such grubby fingernails.

Is she going to tell me I'm adopted? Was the *egg* a donation, too? Are both of my real parents living in Wilmington?

I feel myself getting angry. She picks *now* of all times to drop a bombshell? Now, when my emotions are already so frazzled over Perry?

"Am I adopted?" I ask, crossing my arms. "Is that it?"

"Don't be ridiculous, Ruthie. I've never lied to you

about your birth."

"What *have* you lied to me about?"

My mother's left eyebrow shoots up. I set my jaw defiantly. She takes a deep breath and says, "I never lied. I just never told you the whole truth."

"About what?"

"About the day you were born."

A jolt of electricity zaps my chest.

"Fay!"

At that exact moment, Mrs. Latanza, President of the Odessa Homeowner's Association, enters our yard through the back gate. Her yellow hair is pushed back by a floral headband and hairsprayed into a flip. My whole life, I've never seen her in pants. Today, true to form, she wears a belted gingham dress with white pumps.

"I thought I heard voices back here," she says.

"Peg." Mom eyes her suspiciously.

Mrs. Latanza says, "Betty Fannerife told me Martha was in town, but I had no idea what she was up to!"

Mom leans down and pinches back more cilantro.

"Is this a *major* renovation?" Mrs. Latanza asks, hopeful.

Mom says, "I have no idea what it is."

"Martha looks fabulous, doesn't she?"

"Yes. Fabulous." My mom's fingernails, I notice, are totally green.

Glancing at the open gate, I barely conceal my impatience

when I say, "Maybe you could come back later, Mrs. Latanza, when Aunt Marty is finished."

"Oh, I will," she says. "The whole town has been waiting for this."

With a wiggle of her fingers, Mrs. Latanza says goodbye and exits the same way she came in.

"The nerve of that woman," Mom says. "She thinks she owns this town."

"Yes, well—"

"As if it's my civic duty to maintain my home the way she'd like it to be! Who does she think sh—"

"Mom!"

Startled, Mom glares at me.

"What *about* my birth?" I ask.

"Oh, yes. Where was I?"

I groan. "You were ready to tell me about your lie."

"I never lied to you, Ruthie. I just never told you the whole truth."

"MOM!"

"Okay, okay."

Mom swallows. I try to, but my mouth is spitless.

"I said I was alone that day," Mom begins. "I wasn't."

"My father was there?"

"No. Martha was."

The electric current now shoots down my legs.

"Your aunt was my birthing coach," Mom continues.

"She was the only member of my family who didn't disown me for having you."

I *knew* I had a deeper bond with the Goddess of Love than mere aunt and niece! Her face was probably the first face I saw as I entered the world. Maybe I imprinted on her, like those ducklings who think a dog is their mother when a dog is the first animal they see after they're hatched.

"Did Aunt Marty, by any chance, *carry* me to you the moment I popped out?" I excitedly ask my mother.

Mom doesn't respond and gives me an exasperated look. Which exasperates me, too. Why can't she ever tell me what I want to hear when I want to hear it?

"Is that the big secret?" I ask, incredulous.

My mother's nostrils flare. "She left."

"What do you mean, she *left*?"

"Marty moved to New York to become Martine."

I wait. "And?"

"And the last time I saw her, I told her I never wanted to see her again."

"*That's* it?" My eyes bug out of my head. "You haven't spoken to your sister in fourteen years because she *moved*?"

"Three years," Mom corrects me. "We spoke that weekend in New York. Which cemented my feelings about her. Martha married Richard, told everyone her name was Martine, became someone I don't even recognize, thinks she's an *expert* on men, for heaven's sake, and left me in

Odessa with a baby and two parents who wouldn't speak to me."

"Your parents wouldn't speak to you?" How did I miss out on *that* little tidbit of info?

Again, Mom shoots me an annoyed look. Which, again, annoys me, too.

"Martha decided she wanted to be someone else," Mom says, "so she *became* someone else."

"So?"

"You can't just *decide* to be someone else!"

"Why not?"

My mother's face goes blank for a moment, then she juts out her chin. "What kind of sister turns her back on the one person who needs her most?"

"Me?" I ask.

"No! *Me*."

I roll my eyes. "You didn't expect your sister to live with you forever, did you, Mom?"

My mother's arched eyebrow seems to ask, *Whose side are you on?* She says, "Of course not." Then she adds, "She did say she'd stick around. At least live nearby. But she left."

Aunt Marty living in Delaware? That, I could not wrap my mind around. It threw the planets out of alignment. It disrupted the natural order of the universe.

Tucking her chin into her chest, my mother mumbles something else.

"Come again?" I say.

Quietly, she repeats, "There is one more small thing."

My stomach muscles involuntarily tense. "The big question Aunt Marty is going to ask me?"

"Remember I told you we lived in an apartment above Taylor's?" Mom says.

"We *didn't* live above Taylor's?"

"We did."

"Is Aunt Marty going to ask me about Taylor's?"

"Let me talk, Ruthie," Mom says testily.

Trying to relax my abs, I shut my mouth and let my mother let it all out.

"Those first few years, when you were little, were really hard," she says. "We lived in that tiny apartment, all alone, until your grandparents passed away."

"Uh-huh."

"After that, you and I moved back home."

"Yeah."

So far, my mother hasn't told me anything I haven't heard before. I never knew my grandparents, so I wasn't sad when they died two months apart—one from colon cancer, the other from a broken heart (so they say). Mr. Arthur moved into the house a few months after we did. About the time Perry and I first splashed around in his backyard pool.

"So, what's the small thing, Mom?"

She inhales. "The house."

"This house?"

"Technically, my parents left the house to Martha."

My mouth opens and closes like a goldfish's. "This is Aunt Marty's house?"

Now I understand why the Odessa Homeowner's Association refused to let Mom join up. She isn't a homeowner!

"My parents wanted to punish me for having you," Mom says, "but Martha wouldn't let them. She's let us live here rent-free all these years."

"Wow!"

Mom clucks her tongue. "There's a lot you don't know about your aunt."

"Like what?"

"Like—" Mom looks at me long and hard. I feel my heart pounding. My tongue becomes a dry piece of sandpaper in my mouth. At long last, I will know the whole story.

"Are you wearing *makeup*, Ruthie?"

"Don't change the subject, Mom."

"I'm quite sure I told you gloss only."

"A little mascara and blush! What's the big whoop?"

Mom has that block-of-wood look on her face I've seen a gazillion times. Mules could use lessons from *her* on stubbornness.

She says, "I won't have you disobeying me just because Martha is here."

"It's a stupid rule. I'm *fourteen*!"

Mom says, "Go wash your face."

Bending down, she turns her attention to the garden.

Swiveling, she turns her *back* on me.

"I live in a prison with a warden for a mother!" I say, furiously stomping out through the back gate.

"Don't forget your promise, Ruthie," my mother calls after me. "Remember to say *no*."

PERRY ANSWERS ON THE SECOND KNOCK.

"Oh, hi," he says. A week ago, his emotionless greeting wouldn't have bothered me. Now, it makes me feel like a wad of old gum on my shoe.

"Never mind," I say, turning to leave.

"Wait. What's up?"

Perry looks sleepy. Wrinkled. His shirt smells like popcorn. I want to bury my face in it and let him take me away.

"I've escaped the asylum," I say. "Can I hang out here until the white coats recapture me for dinner?"

He laughs. That crooked tooth makes me weak in the knees.

Perry's mom works at the hospital in Dover. She's a pediatric nurse. Her days are filled with sick children and crying parents. Which is why she saved so hard for Perry's telescope.

"There's got to be something better out there," she said when she gave it to him. "When you find it, will you take me away?"

Mrs. Gould has the right idea.

Perry opens the door wide and I follow him inside.

"I'm watching *Quentin Tarantino's Star Wars* again," he says. "You've seen it, right? He uses action figures and computer animation. Totally dumb, but funny."

I follow Perry into the den. The movie is paused on his TV screen.

"Popcorn?" he asks, plopping down on the couch and tossing me one of the three bags of microwave popcorn that are puffed up on the couch next to him.

"Sure," I say and rip open one of the bags. Buttery steam drifts into my nostrils. It smells like Perry's shirt. I wonder, from now on will the smell of popcorn make me feel in love? Will movie theaters now make me blush?

Perry props his bare feet on the coffee table and hits the

PLAY button on the remote control. I hear a disco version of the *Star Wars* theme. Slipping out of my sandals, I plunk my bare feet on the coffee table, too. Admiring my newly painted toenails, I almost don't notice Perry's feet. Then I do. Is it possible I'd never seen his bare feet before? I must have—at least in the wading pool when we were kids. Now, though, the sight of his feet quickens my pulse. It feels incredibly intimate. Like he's naked. His toes are straight and bony, with fuzzy strawberry-blond hairs. The nails are cut short. There's a sprinkle of freckles on the tops of his feet, his heels are pink. Honestly, I've never seen feet so beautiful.

We watch the movie, munch popcorn.

All of a sudden, Perry tilts his foot to the right and lightly touches the bottom of my foot. It's soft, almost ticklish. I press my foot into his. He doesn't move it. He even presses his foot into mine. Our feet stay together, like hands holding.

I can barely breathe.

The movie continues to play, but I can't hear anything but the whooshing of blood pulsing through my ears.

Then Perry looks at me, and I look at him. We have a *moment.*

We're frozen like that, for what seems like an hour. Touching feet, touching hearts. My chest is on fire. Is this what they mean when they say, "Love hurts"?

"Check this out," Perry says, suddenly breaking the spell.

He moves his foot, grabs the remote, and turns up the volume. "My favorite part," he says.

In a spot-on imitation of Obi-Wan Kenobi, Perry talks over the action figure on-screen, "If you strike me down, I shall become more powerful than you can imagine."

Looking at me, Perry says in a low voice, "The force will be with you always."

Can he tell by my thudding heart that he's probably right?

THE HOUSE IS QUIET WHEN I GET HOME. THE WORKMEN
have all gone. Mr. Arthur is up in his room on the third
floor. Mom is MIA.

"She's hiding like a new kitten," Aunt Marty says.
"She'll only come out when she's good and ready."

"Perfect," I say, grabbing Aunt Marty by the arm. "I
need to talk to you."

We sit. On the *white* couch. Like two grown-ups.

"I'm an idiot," I say.

"What happened?"

Sighing, I confess, "Nothing. I sat next to Perry for two hours watching some dumb DVD and listening to my own heartbeat. He even spooned my foot! But I'm too much of a dunce to make a move. I don't even know *how* to move! What's the rule here? When a guy spoons your bare foot, do you just lay one on him?"

Aunt Marty bursts out laughing.

"It's not funny!" I say. "Perfect Girl probably knows exactly what to do and I'm a moron."

"You, my love, are *brilliant.*"

I roll my eyes.

"Guys feel close by *being* together," she says. "They don't need soul-baring like we do. Be with him while he's doing what he loves, and he'll love you for it."

"I've been with him all his life! That's the problem. I need to figure out how to be with him *differently.* Less friend, more *girl*friend."

"Ah," Aunt Marty says, tapping her chin thoughtfully. "You need a specific plan to rev up his desire."

"Yes! A *Perry* Plan."

She kicks off her shoes, leans back, and tucks her legs beneath her, the way she did when we first met in New York. She looks like a lioness reclining beneath a tree.

"Okay. Let's start with the basics."

"The basics! Thank God!" I clap my hands.

Aunt Marty begins. "Number One, never forg—"

"Yoo-hoo!"

My neck pivots toward the open window. Five heads are crammed into the space, all grinning.

"Martha! Remember me?"

It's Mrs. Fannerife, the woman who now lives above Taylor's—though Taylor's is long gone. She's almost as old as Mr. Arthur—and almost as deaf. I used to wonder why they never hooked up until Mr. Arthur once said, "That Betty Fannerife will talk your ear off!"

Walter Maynard's mom is next to Mrs. Fannerife in the window. She looks like her son. Was there a sale on black-rimmed glasses? Mrs. Latanza is pressing her pointy nose up to the screen. Hovering above all of them are my geography teacher, Mr. Sheeak, and his "friend," Kyle. Both men wear polo shirts with the collars flipped up.

"We've come for the reveal!" Kyle says, practically bursting.

Aunt Marty howls. Without grunting (like my mom does), she rises up from the couch, slips back into her shoes, and glides to the front door.

"Come on in!" she says.

Come *in*? *Hey!* I want to scream, *What happened to the Perry Plan?!*

Kyle pushes in ahead of the group and shrieks.

"Periwinkle blue walls! They're *fab*ulous!"

Aunt Marty steps back and watches our neighbors *ooh* and *aah* over her efforts. I sit slumped on the white couch like a sullen kid.

Mrs. Maynard sighs and says, "Remember your sweet sixteen party in this room, Martha? Well, of course you wouldn't remember."

"I remember," Aunt Marty says.

"That pink dress! My, you were beautiful."

Aunt Marty in a pink dress? In our Odessa living room? No way can I picture that. Obviously, Aunt Marty is having trouble picturing it, too, because she gets a faraway look on her face and says, "That was a lifetime ago."

The group follows my aunt to the back of the house. I get up—not grunting, but moaning impatiently a little—and tag along. Once we enter the sunporch, my jaw drops just as it had when I first came through the front door.

"Goodness," Mr. Sheeak says.

"Finally," adds Mrs. Latanza.

The walls are painted a soft red. "Persimmon," offers Aunt Marty. "Apparently, colors that start with a *P* are my *p*revailing *p*assion," she adds, giggling.

"It's so *p*retty!" Mrs. Fannerife says, one hand on each cheek.

The old Astroturf carpet in the sunporch is gone. The wood floor is painted in a white-and-apple-green checkerboard, the peeling windowpanes have all been scraped, repaired, and repainted. Again, I'm stunned that this transformation happened so fast.

"I bought this daybed in a little antique shop outside of Paris," Aunt Marty says, pointing to the couchlike bed against the wall. Round green pillows dot the back of the bedspread like a row of fluffy limes.

"It must have cost more than the purchase price to ship it home," Mr. Sheeak says.

"It did."

"Feel the thread count," Kyle says, caressing a corner of the sheets. "Ooh la la."

Before that moment, I had no idea what a daybed or a thread count was. Now I know why Aunt Marty's guest bed in New York was so heavenly, and why my Wal-Mart sheets feel like sleeping on newspaper.

"Martha, you've really made this house feel like a home," Mrs. Latanza says. Her eyes tear up.

I can't help but feel a sting. Even though it *looked* like a thrift shop, it's always been home to me.

The seven of us eventually make our way back to the living room where my mother stands, her arms crossed.

"These white couches will be filthy in a matter of days," she says. Her cheeks are flushed and her hair is flat on one side as if she just woke up.

Kyle pipes up, "A little Scotchgard goes a long way."

"Did you see the sunporch, Mom?" I ask.

She asks me, "Did you finish your homework?"

Aunt Marty sighs. "Life is so much more than books."

"I want my daughter to be prepared for *real* life," Mom snorts. "Not some fantasy world where men are dogs."

I gawk. Apparently, my mother reads Aunt Marty's column in the Wawa or the Pathmark, too.

"Men are like dogs, apes, bears, lions, snakes, chameleons, puppies, worms, toads, jackasses, and, if you're really lucky"—Aunt Marty winks at me—"stallions."

Kyle roars. I blush. Mr. Sheeak snickers.

Mom says, "Ruthie, go to your room."

I don't budge. "Why?"

Mrs. Latanza clears her throat. "We should get going," she says.

Mom pointedly doesn't invite anyone to stay. Our neighbors mumble good-byes and slither out the front door. Outside, I hear Mrs. Maynard say, "I bet that pink dress could fetch megabucks on eBay now that Martha is famous."

The three of us stand in our new living room, eyeing one another, not saying a word. Suddenly, Aunt Marty turns to me and asks, "Want to take a drive, Ruthie?"

My eyes dart from my mother's stone will to her sister's stone face.

"We'll pick up something for dinner in Middletown," Aunt Marty adds.

Is *this* the question I promised to say no to? I hope so.

"Yes," I say, throwing my shoulders back, feeling utterly furious with my mother for being so . . . so . . . *her.*

"I'd love to take a drive."

"Ruthie!" Mom's tone could cut glass.

"We'll only be gone a few minutes," Aunt Marty says, grabbing her car keys. "Ready, Ruthie?"

"Yes," I say again. My heart pounds with the power of that little word. "Yes, yes, yes."

I take a defiant step toward the door. Mom glares. Aunt Marty picks up her purse. I follow her as Mom storms out of the room.

AUNT MARTY'S CAR SMELLS LIKE HER—RICH, EXOTIC,
well traveled. The leather seat embraces me with warmth
while the cool air-conditioning blasts my face. We hit a pot-
hole, but I don't feel a thing. Except, of course, the thudding of my heart. What does Mom expect me to do? Sit
home and rot with her? No way!

"You were saying?" I say.

"Saying?"

"The Perry Plan!"

"Ah, yes." Aunt Marty smiles at me. "Really, Ruthie, there's only one major thing you need to know about attracting guys."

I rotate as far as the seat belt will let me. Aunt Marty turns onto Main Street and heads for Middletown. If Odessa had one, I'm sure she would drive in the fast lane.

"You have the power to *teach* a guy how to treat you. The way you act will determine how *he* acts. So, if you want Perry to start treating you like his girlfriend instead of his pal, act like a sensual being."

"Sensual being," I repeat, without a clue how to actually become one.

"I'm not talking about sex," she adds. "Sensuality and sexuality are two very different things. Sensuality is the way you feel about yourself. It's *confidence*. Sex is a whole other matter. Teenage sex is always a disaster. Why put yourself through it? I guarantee, you'll never regret waiting. But you almost certainly will regret it if you don't."

I nod. Even the thought of having sex with Perry Gould makes me blush persimmon.

"What you need to do with Perry," Aunt Marty says, "is change your loop."

"My loop?"

"Any relationship between two people is a loop," she explains. "Both sides respond to each other and keep the loop of their relationship going. If you act differently, your loop will change. The relationship will change. With Perry, you need to step out of the friendship loop and create a *girl*-friendship loop."

"How do I do that?" I ask.

Without hesitation, she says, "Start at the *bottom*."

WALTER MAYNARD, MY GEEKY NEIGHBOR, STARES OPENLY.
Even the school bus driver's eyes pop out of his head. The
next morning, as I swing into the seat next to Perry, he says,
"Your shirt is unbuttoned."

"I know." I try to sound mature, confident. Sensual. Yes,
sensual.

"I'm not kidding, Ruthie. I can see your bra."

"I *know*." Truth be told, it's all I can do to keep from flinging my arms up in front of my chest. But what else can I do? How am I going to change our loop and encourage Perry to view me in a whole new light if I wear my same old clothes?

The night before, on the way to Middletown, Aunt Marty elaborated on the best way to rev up my sensuality and arouse the, um, *stallion* in Perry Gould.

"Always wear silk underpants," she advised.

I laughed. "That's what you mean by 'starting at the bottom'?"

"Yes. Silk underpants make you feel like you're harboring a delicious secret. Which gives you confidence. And *confidence* is the true aphrodisiac."

"Aphro . . . huh?"

"Anything that awakens desire," she replied.

"Got it."

Of course, I don't own any silk underpants. My "lingerie" drawer is full of white cotton. With pink flowers. Which are about as sexy as a baked potato. Definitely not the confidence booster I need to transform my loop with Perry into something more *equine*.

The closest I can get to a "delicious secret" is to color a white bra with a black Sharpie marker. That morning, just before I got to the bus stop, I unbuttoned the top of my shirt so Perry could view the brand-new me.

"Is the buttonhole too big?" he asks, his eyes still bugging out of his head. "Is that the problem?"

Moistening my lips, I ask, "Wanna hang out on your roof tonight? After dark?"

Perry's mouth hangs open. "My *roof*? What is wrong with you, Ruthie? If you don't button up, you're going to get sent home. The principal will never let you wear that. How did your mother let you out of the house? What were you thinking?"

So far, the "Perry Plan" isn't going well. And it's embarrassing!

"What are *you* staring at?" Perry sneers at Walter Maynard, who is turned all the way around in his seat. Walter doesn't stop staring until I hold my backpack up to my front.

Next to me in the cramped seat, Perry fishes through his pack and pulls out a little gold pin.

"Here," he says. "It's stupid, but it'll work."

Perry hands me the pin he received as a finalist in last year's Science Fair. It's in the shape of a moving atom and says, SCIENCE IS A BLAST!

"But—" I say.

"Believe me, Ruthie, you don't want to get off the bus looking like that."

Sighing, I button my shirt. And I wear Perry's pin. Close to my heart.

"Thanks," I say. Then, leaning back against the seat, I smell Perry's smell. It's a combination of herbal shampoo, sunscreen, and something I can't quite identify. The shavings from a pencil sharpener? A new textbook? Stardust? Whatever it is, I shut my eyes and inhale.

That's when it happens again. *Thwang.* My heart beats into his atomic pin. The back of my neck feels like it's being tickled. I can't stop smiling. Before I can control it, I fall more in love than ever.

"What's all over your teeth?" Celeste asks after *third* period, after I stood in front of health class reciting the ten myths of an STD, read from Anne Frank's diary in English class, and passed Perry in the hall, smiling alluringly.

"My teeth?" I gulp.

"Is that *blood*?" Celeste reaches into a side pocket of her pack and hands me a mirror.

Horrified, I see that the super-lustrous, extra-long-wearing Race Car Red lip crème—that Mom would freak out if she saw—has vanished from my lips and settled into the cracks between my teeth.

"It's not supposed to do that," I say weakly, running my tongue back and forth.

Celeste stares. "What is *up* with you?"

"Nothing." My gums have now taken on a rosy hue. Digging a tissue out of my pack, I rub my teeth and gums hard. The lipstick comes off, but the tissue dissolves in my mouth, sticking to my lips. "What's *wong* with a *wittle* makeup?" I say, spitting tiny wads of wet Kleenex into the air.

"Since when do you wear bright red lipstick?"

"Since now." My voice is so Minnie Mouse I don't even believe me.

Celeste raises one eyebrow, examines me. "Is 'Auntie Martine-on-Men' behind this? And, by the way, when are you going to let us meet the diva herself?"

"Behind *what*?" I ask, completely ignoring the second question. "Aren't you going to be late for class?"

"It's *lunch*, Ruthie. What is wrong with you?"

"Wrong? What could possibly be wrong with wanting to update my look?"

Celeste snorts. "Since when do you have a *look*?"

Frankie spots us across the quad and gallops over. She says, "Guess who I just saw talking to Perfect Girl?"

"Who?" I ask, my heart sinking.

"Your sympathy friend."

Celeste scoffs. "Yeah, like he could get *her*."

"Perry's *not* my sympathy friend," I say, stamping my foot. Then I ask Frankie, "What were they talking about?"

She shrugs.

Celeste asks, "If he's not your sympathy friend, what is he?"

I say, "Is that a poppy seed in your teeth?"

Clearly, I can only change one relationship loop at a time.

The next day, I decide not to brush my hair so I'll have the "wild and tousled" style I saw on the last cover of *Fabrique*.

Only, when I see Frankie, she hands me her comb and says, "Be careful not to disturb any birds that might be living in there."

The day after that, in an attempt to inspire Perry to treat me like a girlfriend instead of a friend, I suggest he may want to pay for my slice at Odessa Pizza after school. He suggests that I may want to kiss his butt.

The Perry Plan is *not* going well.

To make matters worse, Mom clings to me like Saran Wrap every moment I'm home. I think she even sits in front of my closed bedroom door at night, knitting, just in case Aunt Marty sneaks upstairs and actually talks to me. Last night, I woke up and heard the *click, click* of knitting needles. It's *so* annoying. It's like she thinks Aunt Marty and I are going to elope.

No, the Perry Plan is not going well at *all*. My old loop is beginning to feel like a rope around my neck.

Time is running out.

School will be over soon. Is Perry going to ask Perfect Girl to the Farewell Dance on the last night of school? Will they hook up at the Peach Blossom Parade?

I have a stomachache.

There's only one thing to do. One thing I *can* do. While Mr. Arthur watches an old *M*A*S*H* rerun, and Mom sits in the living room knitting (*click, click*), I tiptoe through the kitchen and sneak around the back way onto the sunporch.

"Are you busy Saturday?" I quietly ask Aunt Marty, shutting the door.

"Busy?" She laughs. "Yes, I thought I'd watch more paint dry."

"Good," I whisper. "I need a ride into Dover. But there's one tiny little catch. We have to leave *early*."

IT'S THE SMELL OF CINNAMON AND BUTTER. OR THE
pounding musical beat, or the cool air on my skin. Just being
in Dover Mall fills me with happiness.

Aunt Marty and I left before Mom woke up. Which is
exactly the way I planned it. I'd much rather leave a note
than hear her spout a million reasons why going to the mall
will ruin my life.

We stopped for a leisurely breakfast along the way. I had pancakes; Aunt Marty had an egg white omelet with tomatoes. We both drank coffee and cracked jokes and whispered comments about the man in the next booth with the multiple tattoos. Just like we were mother and daughter. Which I wished we were.

"Don't say that," Aunt Marty said, when I let it slip.

"It's true," I said.

"You only think it's true."

"What's the difference?" I asked.

She reached across the table and took my hand. "Fantasy versus reality, my love." Then she asked for the check.

Now we're standing near the Sunglass Hut on the ground floor of Dover Mall. I have twenty-two dollars and seventeen cents in the pocket of my jeans—barely enough to buy anything and it's taken me three months to save it. Still, it's plenty to buy the one thing I need to launch Perry and me into a brand-new loop.

"Where to?" asks Aunt Marty.

"Follow me," I say. Together, we take the escalator up and turn right at the first corner. There, in front of us, is the one stop I need to rev up the Perry Plan: Victoria's Secret.

The store reeks of perfume and powder. My eyes water, and my nose runs the moment I walk into the pink paradise.

Aunt Marty beams. She races ahead, as if she already knows her favorite section. Me, I wander through the demi cups, push-ups, bustiers, corsets, slimmers, enhancers, and enough racy lingerie to outfit the MTV awards show. I feel overwhelmed. The perfume gives me a headache. All I want is a pair of simple silk underpants so I can have a delicious secret—one that Perry Gould can't wait to reveal.

"The silk underwear section, please," I say, when a saleswoman approaches me. She has long blond hair and boobs too big for her tiny body. Her name tag reads, LILAH. Of course her name is Lilah! It's so . . . so . . . exotic. Unlike *Ruthie*, which is so . . . so . . . *not*. Or *Ruth* (ugh!), which sounds like I should have a walker and my teeth in a glass by the bed.

Lilah laughs. "The whole store is the silk underwear section."

"Oh."

"Bikini? Boyshorts? Hipsters? Thong? V-string?"

"V-string?" It sounds painful.

Reaching into a rack of leopard-print panties, she pulls out a tiny triangle of fabric dangling with shoelaces.

"Bikini," I say fast. "Nothing too skimpy. And nothing more than twenty-two dollars and seventeen cents."

"Our superlong thong conforms to your body, doesn't constrict."

"Does it still disappear up your butt?" I ask.

Reluctantly, Lilah nods.

"Bikini," I say. "Pink."

"Lace?"

"A little."

"High cut?"

"Sure."

"Cotton crotch?"

"Definitely."

"Satin waistband?"

"Why not?"

"Ruthie!"

In unison, Lilah and I swing our heads toward the entrance. There, my first-best friend and my second-best friend come bounding toward me. I blink twice, certain I'm seeing a mirage.

"Surprise!" Frankie says, bouncing up and down.

I blink again. They don't go away.

"How did you know I was here?" I finally ask, stunned.

"Your mom told us."

I swallow. "My mom told you I was in Victoria's Secret?"

"No, silly," Frankie says. "She told us you were at the mall. We've been looking all over for you."

"She also said you need to get your butt home," Celeste says. "Though I believe she used the term 'ass.'"

"My mother said *ass*?" Now I gulp. For the first time in my life, I'm glad my mother refused to buy me a cell phone. It would be ringing endlessly now.

Lilah impatiently asks, "What size?"

Frankie laughs. "Yeah, Ruthie. What size *is* your ass?"

"Ruthie?" I hear a voice behind me.

Like the Red Sea parting, the racks of underwear seem to float aside to make room for Aunt Marty. She smiles serenely, even after Frankie bursts into hysterical giggling. Celeste, acting all mature, holds her hand out and says, "You must be Martine."

"I'm Ruthie's aunt Marty," Aunt Marty says, shaking Celeste's hand.

Celeste adds, "You look so much better than your picture in *Fabrique*."

"Thank you," Aunt Marty replies. "I think."

Lilah says, "Oh my God. It's you. I read you every month! I can't believe you're in Dover!"

"Sometimes I can't believe it, either."

Frankie, still tittering, elbows me.

"Oh yeah," I say, "this is Frankie."

Blushing, Frankie over-shakes Aunt Marty's hand. With the four of us chest deep in underwear, I say, "I'm almost done here. We can go soon."

"Go?" Aunt Marty asks.

Like ducklings imprinted on her, Celeste and Frankie echo, "Go?"

Even Lilah says, "Go? You just got here!"

"Well . . . I—"

What can I say? That I came for delicious-secret

underpants so I could bring out the stallion in science-geek Perry Gould? I'd rather wear baggy-assed, flowered, little-girl briefs for *life*.

"I guess we can stay a few more minutes," I say lamely.

Aunt Marty scoffs. "Nonsense! Now that we're all here together, let's go *mad*."

"Yes! Let's!" Celeste sidles up to Aunt Marty. *My* aunt Marty, who says, "Buy whatever you want, girls. It's on *me*."

The next thing I know, my best friends are squealing like piglets. Lilah steps on my toe to get closer to Aunt Marty's credit card. I stand there, with my mouth open, wondering if Perfect Girl is over at Perry's house this very minute spooning his foot . . . and very possibly other body parts.

"Um, my mom is freaking out. I have to get home."

Aunt Marty rolls her eyes. "You left her a note, right?"

"Right."

"She knows you're with me, right?"

"Right."

"So, what's the problem?"

What's the *problem*?! How can I begin to state how many problems have now invaded my life? My feelings for Perry are a secret. My mother thinks her sister is a black widow spider. Perfect Girl keeps flashing her disgusting dimples at my future boyfriend. My underwear is mortifying. When a guy spoons my foot, I freeze into an ice sculpture. And my father is a wiggly thing with a tail!

"Nothing," I say.

"Good. Now have a good time, Ruthie. I'll handle your mother."

What else can I do?

I join the other ducklings and go *mad*.

THE WHOLE DAY IS SURREAL. CELESTE, FRANKIE, AND I can't stop giggling. We buy Ipex demis, T-shirt bras, baby-dolls, boxers, and enough silk underpants to go a full two weeks without doing laundry. Plus, Aunt Marty's panty raid is only the beginning. Her platinum credit card is swiped through cash registers so often I'm surprised its magnetic tape doesn't raise a white flag in surrender. We hit The Body

Shop, the Gap, Tower Records, Banana Republic, and the new Club Monaco store Mom won't even let me enter. ("Those clothes are too old for you. They're all *black*.")

"This is so fun!" Aunt Marty yelps. "I feel like I have three daughters."

With shopping bags puffed out from each arm like water wings, I'm too excited to feel jealous. Aunt Marty's personality is large enough to share. And, though I know I'll have hell to pay when I get home, I feel so happy to hang out in the mall with my best friends and my awesome aunt—just like a normal girl.

"Henry?" Aunt Marty is on her cell while we wait for Celeste's mom at the mall's Information Booth. "I'm in Dover, Delaware. Yes, *Delaware*. What's the best restaurant in town?"

"Who's Henry?" Celeste asks me. I shrug.

"He's the food critic at *Fabrique*," Aunt Marty answers, cupping her hand over the phone. "Henry knows every hot spot in America."

Of course she would call New York to find out where to eat in Delaware. It's so . . . so . . . *her*.

"Le Bistro? Bay Road? Order the salmon almondine? Got it, Henry. You're a love." With a kiss-kiss into the phone, Aunt Marty hangs up.

"A bistro!" Frankie chirps. "How New York!"

"Isn't it French?" I ask.

"Even better!"

115

Celeste's mom dashes up to the booth.

"Sorry I'm late," she says, breathless. "Oh hi, Ruthie!"

Mrs. Serrano kisses my cheek. Then she hugs her daughter and Frankie. Celeste's mom is as different from my mom as two mothers can be. Celeste and her mom are *friends*. When Celeste turned fourteen, her mother took her to the gynecologist to discuss birth control. On my fourteenth birthday, Mom asked me if I wanted to rent *The Little Mermaid* again.

"This is my aunt Marty," I say.

Mrs. Serrano puts her shopping bags on the floor and takes Aunt Marty's hand. "I feel like I know you. Celeste has talked about you nonstop since you came to town."

She *has*?

Without missing a beat, Aunt Marty kisses Mrs. Serrano on both cheeks and replies, "Ruthie told me all about your lovely Celeste."

I *did*?

"I'd like to take the girls out to dinner," Aunt Marty says. "Would that be all right with you?"

"Of course!"

"I promise to have Celeste home by, say, nine?"

"Perfect."

Nine? Mom will be slumped over from a heart attack by then.

While Frankie calls her mom for permission, Celeste excitedly shows her mother her Victoria's Secret haul. Mrs.

Serrano is as excited to see Celeste's Ipex demi as Celeste was to buy it.

My stomach lurches. I pull Aunt Marty aside.

"I can't go out to dinner," I say quietly.

"Why not?"

"Mom is already pissed."

"That's ridiculous."

"I know. But that's the way she is."

"I'll deal with her." Aunt Marty takes her phone out again.

I sigh.

"It'll be fine, Ruthie. You're allowed to have fun."

Once again I'm in awe. How do you become the type of person who charges headlong into life assuming everyone will get out of your way?

"I'm in," Frankie squeals, putting her phone back in her purse.

"Me, too," says Celeste, kissing her mother good-bye.

I glance at Aunt Marty, who is listening to Mom St. Helens erupting in her ear. Still, she flashes me a thumbs-up. Swallowing, I take a deep breath and say, "Me, *three*."

LE BISTRO IS THE MOST GROWN-UP RESTAURANT I'VE
ever been to. What am I saying? It's the *only* grown-up
restaurant I've been to. It's dark inside even though it's still
light outside, there are more booths than tables, more wait-
ers with accents than waitresses with name tags, and the
menu doesn't have a single color photo.

"A Cosmopolitan, please," Aunt Marty murmurs to the dark-haired waiter as he tucks us into a corner booth.

"Make that two," I say, flipping my hair. Whatever a Cosmopolitan is. It just sounds so . . . so . . . *cosmopolitan*, which is what I need—some city chic to counteract my terminal country-bumpkiness.

Aunt Marty grins and says, "Three virgin Cosmos, please. And one with a bit more experience."

The waiter nods and leaves.

We open our menus and disappear behind them. Everything is in French.

"The *haricots verts* sound fabulous, don't they, Martine?" Celeste says, trying to appear older than she is.

Aunt Marty smiles. "Yes, I love green beans."

"I bet this sea bass with *beurre meunière* is scrumptious," Frankie says.

"Bear manure?" I quip. *"Merveilleux!"*

We all crack up, elbow each other in the ribs, throw our heads back against the black leather of the booth. I run my fingers lightly down my neck the way I'd seen Aunt Marty once do.

"On Henry's orders, I'm having the salmon almondine. Appetizer size. But have anything your hearts desire," Aunt Marty says airily.

At the mention of my heart's desire, I flash on Perry Gould. But, just as quickly, I recover. "The salmon sounds yummy." The closest I've ever come to eating salmon before was StarKist tuna. "Appetizer size for me, too."

"Us, too," Frankie and Celeste chime in.

Our Cosmopolitans arrive, and Aunt Marty tells the handsome waiter what we want. He says, "Excellent choice."

We beam and settle into the cushy leather seats. The spindly stemmed glasses of our Cosmos stand like four sparkling rose-hued sentries, guarding Wonderland.

"Vodka, triple sec, lime juice, and cranberry juice," says Aunt Marty.

My eyes get wide. "In *mine*," she adds. "Yours are probably jazzed-up ginger ales."

I take a sip. It's the best ginger ale *ever.*

"To us." Aunt Marty raises her glass.

"To us," we repeat. How amazing is it that Aunt Marty considers us an *us*? I feel so high my ginger ale could have been champagne. In fact, I feel wild—empowered with Goddesslike potential.

"Now that you have our undivided attention," I say to my beautiful aunt, "will you teach us how to turn men into quivering masses of adoring goo?"

Aunt Marty bursts out laughing. "Men? You're fourteen."

"Okay, *boys*," I say. "After tonight, we want to become *Delaware's* Goddesses of Love."

120

Celeste and Frankie excitedly bob their heads up and down.

Aunt Marty narrows her eyes. "Shall I open Martine's bags of tricks and share them with you girls?"

We bounce up and down on the soft leather seat.

Coyly, she asks, "Do I dare?"

"Yes! Yes!"

"Can you handle the *truth*?"

The three of us are ready to burst. Aunt Marty sips her Cosmo, runs her fingers down her neck. It feels like a month before she says, "Okay. I think you're ready to enter Martine's Magic Kingdom."

Like little kids, we clap our hands. And our "teacher" begins the one class in which I'll pay full attention: *Boys 101.*

"Lesson Number One: Forget all that Mars and Venus crap. Guys and girls are *exactly* the same. We only *express* it differently. Deep down, everyone wants one thing from the person they love: to be *accepted* for who they really are. We all yearn to be known, to be emotionally naked in front of someone and not rejected because of it. That's what makes us feel truly loved. That's what we all crave. And that's where most girls fall down on the job. May I?"

My aunt reaches across the table for a piece of baguette. She rips the inside out of it and eats only the crust. Celeste, Frankie, and I gut our bread as well.

"Lesson Number Two: Accepting your boyfriend for who he truly is, instead of wishing, manipulating, forcing, begging, tricking him into becoming the guy you *want* him to be, is the formula for a happy relationship. Choosing a guy for his 'potential' is a recipe for disaster."

An older gentleman eating alone at a table next to ours must have overheard because he catches Aunt Marty's gaze and winks. In true Goddess fashion, she smiles slyly and winks right back.

"Next," she leans close to us, "never forget that a guy will tell you exactly who he is and what he wants right off the bat. You have to learn how to *hear* him. You also have to believe what you hear. For instance, he won't come out and say, 'I'll cheat on you the moment I have the chance,' but he will say, 'Rock stars have it made.' He won't say, 'I don't want to talk about it,' but he'll instantly change the subject. He may not say the words, 'I'm sorry,' but he'll buy you flowers. *We* are the ones who demand specific words. Who says words are the only way to communicate?"

New York's Goddess of Love spreads her pink linen napkin on her lap and smoothes it flat with her hands. Like Mini-Martys, we do exactly the same thing. In the soft light of Le Bistro, my aunt looks like a movie star.

"Love," she says, caressing the glass stem, "is what you feel when someone makes you happy with *yourself.* Show a man how to love *himself* and he will adore you. Love is the ultimate ego trip."

Caressing my glass stem, I dramatically sip my virgin Cosmo.

"Lesson Number Four: Guys don't fear commitment, they fear *entrapment*. They *want* girlfriends, but not girlfriends who act like their mothers. He wants you in his life, but he doesn't want you to *devour* his life. Guys don't need a mind-meld like we do. They don't believe that two halves make a whole. Instead, it's more like two wholes make a couple. Which is a much healthier way to view relationships."

The appetizer-sized portions of salmon almondine arrive. The warm smell of butter and roasted almonds hangs over the table like a soft blanket. Aunt Marty speaks between bites.

"Never forget that men *live* to make us happy. When you are happy, he is happy."

The waiter appears and asks, "Everything okay?"

Okay? I want to tell him I'm having the time of my life. Aunt Marty lightly touches his hand and coos, "This is the best meal I've had all evening." He laughs, raises his eyebrows at her, refills our water glasses. The moment he leaves, she says, "See? He's happy because we are happy."

She takes another bite, chews, swallows, then says, "Women spend so much time griping about all the ways men aren't perfect, they eventually give up trying. Who wants to feel like a failure? Let your man know how much he pleases you and he'll trip over himself to keep it going."

Again, I think about Perry. Had I ever let him know how much he pleases me?

"Isn't that a little *unfeminist*?" I ask.

"Feminist *schmem*inist. I'm a humanist. I'm a *practicalist*! I'm not saying you should do what your boyfriend wants to do if it's dangerous or disgusting. I'm not suggesting you sacrifice yourself for him. Never. No way. All I'm saying is this: If you want him in your life, let him be who he is. And join him while he's being *himself*."

"What about sex?" Celeste blurts out. Aunt Marty leans her head back against the booth, sighs.

"Ah, yes. Sex."

We hold our breath. Aunt Marty takes her time. I can't help but admire her again. She knows how to work a room. Even if that "room" is three teenagers who know next to nothing.

"Girls make the mistake of thinking *sex* is the way to a boy's heart," Aunt Marty says finally. "It isn't. It's the way to another organ. *Period*. Girls who have sex too soon regret it because they rarely get what they want: love. Never forget that guys *separate* sex and love; girls confuse the two. Besides, it's the girl who takes on all the risk—pregnancy, diseases. Why do it? Believe me, sex is not worth the risk until much later. Until you're in a committed relationship—

both heart and soul. Trust me. That's the truth."

"We believe you," Celeste says. Frankie and I nod.

Aunt Marty peers into my eyes. "Shall we order dessert?"

Dessert? Could this evening get any better?

Aunt Marty orders four individual chocolate soufflés for us and an espresso for herself. We devour our desserts (Aunt Marty eats exactly three bites), melt into the leather booth, and bask in the afterglow of Aunt Marty's advice. I feel more than grown-up; I feel *mature.* Confident. Womanly, even. Dare I say it, I feel the seed of Goddessdom blossoming within my soul. Perry Gould will soon be putty in my hands. He'll be a quivering mass of goo, he'll worship at the altar of Ruth, he'll—

"What's wrong?"

Aunt Marty's beautiful, serene face suddenly disintegrates into sloppy tears and snot.

"Who am I trying to kid?" she blubbers.

I don't know where to look.

"Another Cosmo, Martine?" Alarmed, Celeste pats her shoulder.

"I don't know anything about men! I don't know a thing about life!"

"What do you mean?" Frankie yelps. Before our admiring eyes, my blueprint of a Goddess crumbles like French bleu cheese. It's like running into one of your teachers in the

125

mall while he's eating a bean burrito and wearing short shorts. It's all wrong, and once you see it, you can never *un*see it.

"Richard left me a month ago." Aunt Marty weeps. "He's been seeing another woman for a year and a half. And she's *older* than I am! He actually told me that she *understands* him. Can you believe it? I mean, how clichéd is that?"

My eyes open wide. "But I saw the way he looked at you!"

"He now looks at someone else that way," she says through her tears.

Celeste, I notice, is still patting Aunt Marty's shoulder.

"I'm a total fraud," Aunt Marty says through her tears. "All I can do is spout platitudes that my editor writes for me."

"You're not spouting plati . . . whatevers," Frankie says, reaching past me to pat Aunt Marty's other shoulder.

"Plati*tudes*," she blubbers. "Stupid, meaningless sayings."

I gulp. "You mean, men *don't* live to make us happy?"

Not to be heartless, but the last thing I need to hear is that my man expert is having man trouble. I'm not proud of this, but I find myself wondering if the "Perry Plan" will fall to pieces if "Martine on Men" really *doesn't* know men.

Like I said, I'm not proud of it.

Aunt Marty sniffs. Truthfully, it doesn't help much. I rummage through my backpack for a tissue.

"That's why I'm here in Odessa, Ruthie," she continues, her mascara beginning to look very Marilyn Manson. "I've moved out of my apartment. We sold the house in the Hamptons."

"White couches," I whisper to Celeste, desperate to turn the clock back to a time when Aunt Marty knew everything and wasn't all blotchy.

"I had to get away for a while," she says, sniffing hard. I dig deeper for that Kleenex. "Everything in New York reminds me of Richard."

"What about your column? What are we going to read about next month?" Celeste stops patting Aunt Marty's shoulder.

"My editor and I did a bunch of them before I left. Not that anyone will care. As soon as word gets out that I can't even keep a husband happy, who's going to listen to me advise them about men?"

"I will," Celeste says.

"I will, too," Frankie says.

"Me, three," I add sincerely, finally finding a Kleenex and handing it to her.

Aunt Marty blows her nose, then wraps both arms around us and squeezes. "What would I do without my family and friends?"

The waiter swings by our table and asks, "Would you like anything else?"

Aunt Marty smiles, lifts her head, straightens her shoulders, elongates her neck, and states, "No thank you. My life is perfect."

Laughing, the waiter leaves to get the check.

"The one thing I still know for sure," Aunt Marty says, sniffing, "is even when you feel terrified, *act* fearless. People believe what they think they see."

IT'S ABOUT NINE O'CLOCK WHEN WE GET HOME, BUT IT
feels like midnight. The house is nearly dark. A single, dim
light from Mom's bedside lamp drifts eerily through the
upstairs window. As we enter through the front door, Aunt
Marty and I hear Mom's knitting needles clicking from her
bedroom upstairs. The moment the door shuts, the noise
abruptly stops.

"We're home, Mom," I call up the stairs, swallowing hard. The lump in my stomach feels thick and yeasty. Aunt Marty flips on some lights; I stand still, dreading what is about to happen. Suddenly, the floorboards creak and we hear footsteps overhead. My mother, already in her flannel nightgown, slowly descends the stairs.

"Ruthie, go to your room." Her tone is ice. Betrayal has turned her eyes black.

"But, Mom—"

"*Now.*"

I don't dare disobey. Clutching my shopping bags, I bolt for the stairs and run up to my room, loudly shutting the door even though I'm still in the hall. No one told me I had to go *in* my room.

Mr. Arthur, I notice, is peering over the third-floor railing. He looks petrified. Apparently, he's had an earful all evening.

"Who do you think you are?" I hear the quiver in my mother's voice.

Aunt Marty has recovered from her sobfest in Le Bistro. Her tone is as sharp as a hangnail. "Who do *you* think I am, Fay?"

"You can't have my daughter."

"Have her? Like she's a piece of jewelry?"

"You know what I mean." My mother's voice trembles with fear and rage. I don't have to see her to know what she looks like: a Christmas tree in February—hard, prickly needles. "You can't show up and throw your money around and fill my daughter's head with garbage. You can't lure her into your web and make her want to leave me."

"Don't be so melodramatic, Fay," Aunt Marty says.

Now I hear the rustle of Aunt Marty's shopping bags. Looking up, I see that Mr. Arthur is leaning so far over the banister, his thick glasses are nearly hanging off his head. "What'd she say?" he whispers hoarsely to me.

Shrugging my shoulders, I don't speak for fear of missing a word.

"I know why you're here, Martha. You don't fool me. Just because you chose a career over a child doesn't mean you can have mine."

In my head, I hear Aunt Marty's voice: *People believe what they think they see.*

The rustling stops. In fact, it feels like the Earth stops spinning.

"I told you no in New York," my mother says, "and I'll say it again in Odessa. You can't have my daughter. I don't care that you *paid* for my in vitro, as you so ungraciously reminded me three years ago. I don't care that you think you can give her a better life, or that you've let us live here rent-free all these years. She's still *my* daughter and she always will be."

Now, I stop breathing. It feels like the whole house is holding its breath.

"Stop it, Fay," Aunt Marty says quietly. "You're embarrassing yourself."

"With the truth?"

"The truth?" I don't need to see my aunt Marty to know that she's turned around and is flexing her feline claws. "You want the truth, Fay? Yes, it's true that I offered to take Ruthie three years ago. You'd lost your job, and Richard and I thought we could help. But when you said no, we never brought it up again."

My breath is shallow. My head is spinning.

"Look at yourself," Aunt Marty says. "In your pajamas at nine o'clock. You'd think you lived in a nursing home!"

Mr. Arthur, I notice, is also dressed for bed.

Aunt Marty's shopping bags fall to the floor in a loud *thwump*. "You want truth? I'll give you truth. You can't *stand* the fact that I got out of here, and you stayed. I made something of my life, and you never left home. That's what's eating you alive. You're not afraid I'll steal Ruthie, you're afraid she'll *want* to be with me more than you."

"That's ridiculous," Mom says.

"Is it? Look at your life, Fay. You've hidden in this house, wrapped it around yourself like a tattered robe. You could have created a happy life anywhere. Instead, you chose to become an old woman in Odessa. A bitter, suspicious old hag. Is that the example you want to set for your daughter? Do you think that's a role model she respects?"

Aunt Marty pauses. I hear nothing but Mr. Arthur's mouth-breathing.

"You don't hate *me*, Fay. You hate yourself for being such a coward."

My heart leaps into my throat.

"You want Ruthie to respect you?" Aunt Marty continues. "Get yourself a respectable *life*—one that both of you can be proud of. If you don't, *you'll* be the one to push Ruthie so far away from you and Odessa you'll never see her again. *That's* the truth."

Again, I hear the swishing of Aunt Marty's shopping bags as she scoops them off the floor and strides to the sunporch at the back of the house. Her footsteps echo across the hardwood floor. Then she abruptly stops.

"Just so you don't think you're the only one being nailed with honesty tonight, Fay, you should know that Richard left me. Over a month ago, I came home to a letter from his attorney telling me I had six months to find a new apartment and start a new life. He might as well have shot me in the heart. It's already a bloody alimony fight, probably the beginning of the end for 'Martine on Men.' That's *my* reality."

A deafening silence spreads through the whole house.

Her voice shaky, Aunt Marty adds, "For the first time in my life, I couldn't handle being alone. *That's* why I came home. Not to take Ruthie, but to be with the only family I have left."

Mom sighs. "Oh, Martha. Why didn't you tell me?"

Aunt Marty doesn't say anything for the longest time.

Then, in a whisper, she says, "Because the thought of becoming Martha again scares me more than anything."

Aunt Marty doesn't say anything more, but she doesn't need to. I totally understand.

It's nearly eleven o'clock before the familiar creaking of the stairs announces my mother's slow climb up to bed, each step sounding like a sack of flour being tossed to the floor.

"Mom?" I open my door a crack as she walks past.

"Why aren't you in bed?"

"I can't sleep. Are you oka—?"

"You heard, didn't you?"

I nod.

Standing there in the dim hall light, in her flannel nightie, my mom looks like a little kid. At that moment, I feel more love for her than I've felt in a long time. She steps close to me, runs her fingers through my hair.

"Now you know," she says.

Again, I nod. In a quiet voice, Mom says, "It's true, isn't it? What you said the other day. I've been your warden. I've locked you up in my prison."

I don't know what to say. How can I lie? How can I tell the truth? A flood of feelings wash through my heart. After all these years wanting to escape my life, was freedom merely a matter of calling Aunt Marty? Would I really have been able to leave my mom? Perry? Celeste? Odessa? Does the offer still stand? Do I want to go?

My mother moves even closer to me, peers so deeply into my eyes it feels as though she's looking at her own reflection. Taking both of my hands in hers, she says, "When the time comes, I want you to do what you have to do, go where you need to go, okay? Even if you know I'm going to be upset. I want you to live *your* life, Ruthie. Even if it devastates me to lose you. Promise me, okay?"

"Okay," I whisper.

"Promise."

"I promise."

What else could I say?

FOR THE REST OF THE WEEKEND, THE HOUSE IS EERILY quiet. We all stake out safe spaces. Mom in the living room. Aunt Marty on the sunporch. Mr. Arthur on the third floor, and me in my room. The house doesn't smell like fresh paint anymore. But it *feels* like a fresh wound.

"Finish your milk, Ruthie," Mom says to me at dinner.

Aunt Marty isn't there. She said she had to take care of

something in Wilmington, but the stiffness in her voice made me not believe her. I think she just wanted some time alone.

I finish my milk. Mr. Arthur doesn't even mention that milk is Delaware's state beverage the way he does practically every night. Like my mom and me, he chews quietly, then excuses himself from the table and disappears.

Up in my room, my head feels like cotton candy. I don't know what to think. My emotions are on overload. So, I decide to focus on the one thing in my life that makes perfect sense: the Perry Plan. Now I know *exactly* what I have to do.

It's lunchtime at school, and the library is deserted. Except, of course, for Walter Maynard, who's online researching nuclear waste disposal for an extra-credit report. I know this because I sit next to him at the computer bank and he tells me about it while he stares straight at my boobs. Not that I'm wearing my Sharpie bra anymore. But that's not stopping Walter.

"Yucca Mountain can only hold the waste for ten thousand years," he says, eyes shifting from one boob to the other. "What then?"

I cross my arms, face the computer screen, and say, "I can't worry about that now, Walter."

"If we don't worry now, who ever will?"

He has a point. Still, I have work to do. And no way can

I do it at home with a *dial-up* modem. Mom would catch me for sure.

I log on and click until I enter the site I need. Holding my breath, I move the cursor onto the link for the fees and schedules. "Please, God," I whisper, "don't let it be too expensive."

"Expensive?" Walter shoves his glasses up the bridge of his nose. "What price are you putting on a radioactive holocaust?"

Moving my mouse to the PRINT icon, I left click on it. Walter is still staring at me as I get up and walk around the corner to the printer. In a few seconds, it spits out exactly what I need. Adrenaline gushes through my system. It's not going to be easy, but it's definitely doable.

Grabbing the piece of paper, I dash for the door, hoping to make it to the cafeteria before the good food is gone.

"Hey, Ruthie!" Walter shouts after me. "Will I see you on the bus?"

Perry waves at me from across the quad. Instantly, I slow down. I walk *sensuously.* Feeling my delicious-secret underpants, I act fearless even though I feel terrified.

"Hurry up," Perry yells, rolling his eyes.

Inching into Perry's personal space, I force myself to gaze seductively into his eyes. My heart pounds, my eyes water, but no way am I going to blink.

It's now or never.

I can barely breathe.

"You busy Saturday?" I ask, inhaling to steady my quivering knees.

"No. Why?"

Another deep breath. *Suck it up, girl,* I say to myself. *Dive in. Be a goddess. Make your move.*

"We're going to Washington, D.C."

FOR THE FIRST TIME IN MY LIFE, EVERYTHING FEELS EX-
actly right. Except, of course, the big fat lie I tell my mother.

"I'm trying out for the school play."

"A *play*? I had no idea you were interested in acting,"
Mom says.

"I'm not. I'm doing props." *Good one, Ruthie,* I think
smugly.

"Props?"

"You know, setting stuff up. Helping the actors get ready."

"Helping the actors? Isn't that wardrobe?"

Since when does my mother know anything about wardrobe?

"Um, yeah, Mom. But my job would be to handle the props that go *with* wardrobe." I bite the inside of my cheek.

"On a Saturday?"

"It's the only time the auditorium is free."

"They're doing a play this late in the school year?"

"It's for *next* year, really," I say, looking down. "They want us to study it over the summer."

"What play is it?"

"The *school* play."

"What's the name of it?"

"Uh, I forget."

Sweat beads begin to form on my upper lip.

"You forget?"

"Shakespeare, I think. I just remember them saying something about the props being, uh, swords."

Clearly, I have no clue what I'm talking about. And I've already broken Rule Number One of Effective Lying: Keep it simple. Just as it seems my mother's questions will never stop and I'll be forced to break down, crumble to the floor, clutch at her ankles, blurt out the truth, and beg for forgiveness, she stuns me by saying, "Okay."

"Okay?"

"Will you be home for dinner?"

Not even daring to breathe, I quickly sneak the elephant into the living room. "They're feeding us pizzas. I won't be home until seven."

"Seven?"

"No later. Promise," I rasp.

"Okay."

Mom smiles and says, "Marty and I may grab a bite to eat in Middletown."

I stare at her. When you're not looking, people can change right before your eyes.

You know how they say that shoplifting a pack of gum can lead to robbing a convenience store, or smoking cigarettes can lead to smoking pot? Well, I now believe that's probably true because the first big fat lie I told my mother led directly to a bigger fatter lie I told my aunt.

"Your mother said it was okay for you and Perry to hop on a bus to Washington, D.C.?" she asks me, incredulous.

"Yes. Yes, she did."

"The same mother who freaked out when you went to the Dover Mall?"

"That would be her, yes." I swallow, forcing my eyes to stare into Aunt Marty's eyes because "Martine on Men" once said, "It's easy to tell when a guy lies—he simply won't meet your gaze. He'll stare at your forehead, the bridge of your nose, one eyebrow or the other, but he won't look you in the eye." Even though I now know it's a platitude, I can only assume she thinks it's true of fourteen-year-old nieces, too.

"Perry's mother also says it's okay?"

My left eye starts to twitch. "Oh, yes. Yes, she's fine with it."

I have no idea what Perry told his mother but I'm pretty sure it's not even close to the truth, the whole truth, and nothing but. Aunt Marty, being Aunt Marty, handles things way differently than my mother.

"You're lying to me, aren't you?" she says flatly.

"Lying?" (I break Rule Number Two of Effective Lying: Never repeat the question in a lame attempt to stall for time.)

"Lying, you know, as in not telling the truth."

My mind races, darting from one implausible explanation to another. Finally, I blurt out the only thing that makes sense: "Yes. I'm lying."

Aunt Marty narrows her eyes. "Knock it off, Ruthie. I don't like liars."

"Sorry." I hang my head, having broken Rule Number Three: Never get busted for telling a lie because it makes you feel like a total heel. All in all, I realize, it's less stressful telling the truth.

"Can I start over?" I ask.

"Please do."

I start over.

"I want to share an amazing experience with the boy that I love."

Saying it out loud almost makes me faint.

"Go on," says Aunt Marty.

"Everything is planned out," I say. "We're going straight there and coming straight home. I'll be back by seven. You don't know me that well, Aunt Marty, but I'm not the type to do anything stupid. Perry isn't, either. We're both good kids, good students. We can handle this. I swear, we can."

As I speak, I see the wheels of her brain turning. "Straight there? Straight back?" she asks.

"Yes."

"You'll be home by seven?"

"Definitely."

Aunt Marty squints at me. She looks at me long and hard. Then she leans over and encircles me with her arms, hugging me tightly.

"You're wrong, Ruthie," she says. "I *do* know you well. You're everything your mother and I dreamed you would be."

For the first time since she arrived, I hug my aunt for as long as I want, unable to wipe the sappy smile off my face.

"I have two conditions, however," my aunt says, pulling away from me. "Number one, take my cell and call me instantly if anything happens. *Anything* at all."

"You got it. What else?"

"Tell your mother the truth."

My shoulders sag. "I can't."

"Look, Ruthie, your mother and I are just finding our way back to each other. The last thing we need is for her to find out you've lied to her and told me the truth."

Now I have no trouble looking Aunt Marty right in the eye.

"I know my mother trusts me. And Perry. She knows I can handle it. But right now, *Mom* can't handle it. She's freaking out because I'm growing up. She would never let me go to Washington, because she's not ready to let go of *me*. She wants to, but she can't. Not yet. And I don't have enough time to wait for her emotions to catch up with what she knows is right."

Flabbergasted, Aunt Marty sits back in her chair. "When did you get so smart?"

I'm a bit stunned, too. It's the first time I've been able to put into words what I've known in my heart all along.

"I know it's wrong to lie," I say. "But in this case, I also know it's right."

Aunt Marty gazes at me a long time before she quietly says, "I never intended to hurt your mother."

"I know."

"Sometimes being yourself means upsetting people who need you to be someone else."

Man, did I know that, too.

"Have a great time with Perry, Ruthie. You deserve it."

Flinging my arms around my aunt, I hug her tight. I feel the softness of her shirt against my cheek. Then I take a deep breath and ask, "Is there any chance you could loan me sixty-five dollars and forty cents?"

THROUGH THE BUS WINDOW, WE BOTH WATCH THE SUN RISE over Appoquinimink Creek. I feel as ecstatic as I am nervous. I can't believe I'm actually doing this. At the same time, I can't believe it's taken me so long.

"I'll pay you back for this," Perry says as we head north.

"I don't want you to pay me back. My aunt gave me the money. I want you to have a fantastic time." Then, my pulse racing, I add, "With me."

• The city bus bumps along Route Thirteen, stops in Boyds Corner, Biddles Corner, St. Georges, and Wrangle Hill. Each stop is little more than an opening and closing of the door. We sit together on the double seat, our denims brushing up against each other with each lurch of the bus. I want to nibble his earlobe, tell him he's my Saturn and I'm his rings. A celestial storm of fright and thrill pulses through every capillary. The musky smell of his hair overwhelms me with feelings of love. Already, it's the most amazing day.

Perry doesn't say a word. I'm tempted to fill the silence with nervous chatter, but I stop myself. Words would ruin the moment. And I want every nanosecond of this day to be burned into my memory forever.

Besides, my lips are so dry, words would only get stuck on the way out of my mouth.

Perfect Girl can have her flawless tan. I have Perry.

Once we transfer to the Greyhound bus in Wilmington, three and a half hours separate us from Washington, D.C. With each passing hour, my buzz level increases exponentially. (I know this because Perry explains that the word *exponential* means a number multiplying itself by itself, and that's exactly what is going on in my adrenaline-flooded body.) By the time the bus driver bellows, "Washington, D.C., the nation's capital, next stop!" we're both shooting sparks off the tops of our heads. Perry leaps to his feet before the bus even comes to a stop.

"Let's jam!" he shouts.

The Greyhound terminal is a block behind the D.C. train station, which is a gorgeous, enormous, bright-white building rising up against the powder-blue sky. Perry and I run for it, unable to keep our feet from flying. The sun feels warm and wet, like the bathroom after a long shower. Perry takes my hand, and it feels so natural, it's as if we were born with our fingers intertwined.

"Look!" he yelps.

The dome of the Capitol Building is visible in the distance. I yelp, too. I want to roll in the green grass across from the station, swing on the branch of a blossoming cherry tree. I want to kiss Perry Gould and whisper, "You are my love."

"I'm starving," Perry says.

It's nearly eleven thirty. We have time for a quick lunch. And, thanks to Aunt Marty, who insisted on giving me a hundred-dollar bill ("Not a loan," she said, "but an *investment* in my brilliant, beautiful niece."), I can afford to pay for it.

"Follow me," I say, not letting go of Perry's hand. I'm prepared. I know exactly where to go.

We circle around to the front of the train station and walk under a chorus line of huge arches that lead inside. As I pull Perry through the heavy brass-handled doors, we both gasp.

"Get *out*." Perry tilts his head up. The sky-high, vaulted

ceiling is a honeycomb pattern of white and gold. It's the most take-your-breath-away sight I've ever seen. Sunlight bursts through the front windows and bounces off the shiny cream-and-maroon marble floor. A two-story circular restaurant sits in the middle of the lobby, surrounded by real trees. The air itself is alive. Important-looking people scurry in and out, dressed in serious black pumps and pin-striped suits. Suitcases roll across the glassy floor. Arrival and departure announcements vibrate through the air.

Once again, my heart clutches with the sense that I was born in the wrong place. I belong in a city with a train station like this! I want *my* air to sparkle.

Suddenly, an image of my mother standing alone and abandoned in her old plaid robe flashes through my head. But I press my eyes closed and erase it. Nothing is going to ruin this amazing day.

"Check this out," I say to Perry, leading him down a polished wood spiral staircase to the floor below the main lobby. There, we're in the middle of a gigantic food court. But it's not like the food court at Dover Mall. It's *gourmet*. There's grilled seafood, a sushi bar, quarter-pound burgers, individual pizzas, pasta, heros, gyros, burritos, freshly baked cookies, smoothies, lattes—anything and everything you could ever want to eat or drink.

"I want to live here," Perry says, grinning.

I want to kiss you, I long to say.

Like two mountain lions stalking a zebra, Perry and I

scope out each mouth-watering possibility before pouncing on Philly cheese steaks. The grilled meat smells irresistible. Perry orders onions with his sandwich. I skip them. No way do I need to worry about my breath with so much else going on. He also insists on paying for lunch.

"It's the least I can do," he says.

The juice from the steak dribbles down my chin, the cheese singes the roof of my mouth. My diet soda, mixed with nerves and excitement, makes me burp nonstop. But I also can't stop smiling.

By noon, stuffed and exhilarated, Perry and I wiggle our way through the crowd to the long escalator leading down into the elegant gray tunnels of the Metrorail. Right on schedule.

Washington's subway is clean and modern, nothing like the old New York City subways I've seen in movies. I mean, there's no graffiti or anything. Everybody is superpolite. When the train is about to enter the station, lights flash on the platform. And the train is so quiet, you'd barely know it arrived. The doors open and close with a *Star Trek*–like *swoosh*.

We grab two seats facing each other. I smell someone's take-out Chinese food. The train hums as it speeds along the track. I've never felt more grown-up in my life. Finally.

According to my research, it'll take about ten minutes to get to the Smithsonian Institution. Which isn't an "institution" at all, but sixteen museums and galleries full of awesome stuff like Dorothy's ruby slippers from *The Wizard of Oz* and the biggest blue diamond in the world.

Plus the one thing Perry has dreamed of seeing for years.

In those few minutes, I look around me. *Will this ever be my life?* I wonder. Will I have the guts to leave Odessa? Again, I ask myself, will I want to leave if everyone I love—except Aunt Marty—lives in or near my hometown?

The Metro comes to a stop so softly I barely feel it. As the doors slide open and we step off the train, I glance at my watch again. Twenty minutes to showtime. No time to waste. There may be a line.

Perry follows me up the escalator steps and we emerge onto a huge rectangle of lawn. The bright sunlight has turned it turquoise. The clear sky is the color of a sapphire. Who needs to see a giant blue diamond when it's such a jewel of a day?

Stopping to check my downloaded map, I look right and left. Pointing, I say, "Over there."

"Wahoo!" Perry gallops across the grass. I bound after him, laughing the entire way. Euphoria hits me like a blast from a fire hose. I feel *free.* Unchained. The prison bars have been opened and I've made my escape.

We take the museum steps two at a time. Then we stop dead. There *is* a line. *Outside.* Security guards are checking everyone's bags before they even let them through the door.

"Oh, no," I groan, looking at my watch again. My pounding heart sinks. We're running out of time.

"We'll make it," Perry says with such calm assurance I totally believe him. Tilting my head back, I feel the sun on my face. For once, I don't care about freckles. I feel absolutely peaceful. It almost freaks me out. It's like I'm in the exact time and place I'm meant to be. My head, body, and soul are all united. There, on the concrete sidewalk, with Perfect Girl miles away and Perry Gould *inches* away, I actually feel . . . *normal.* In this moment, nothing is missing.

"Next."

We make it through the security checkpoint quickly and run inside. Just in time. Everyone is already in the theater. We buy tickets, grab our 3-D glasses, and race through the double doors just before they close. Perry leads me straight to two seats near the front.

"The third row?" I ask. A six-story IMAX movie screen and we were going to sit in the third row?

"Trust me," he says.

I shrug. Why not? Popping the 3-D glasses on my face and leaning back against the soft seat, I crank my neck backward and prepare to be transported.

The lights dim. Away we go.

As soon as the film starts, I'm floating in space. I feel as though I'm right there, in the blackness of outer space, my birth planet brown and blue in the distance. I'm incredibly far from Earth, yet I feel completely at home.

Instantly, I understand why Perry wanted to sit so close. The third row is the ideal distance from the screen. Even though people sit in front of us, our heads are tilted back so far we can't see them. Any farther back in the theater, it would be impossible to avoid seeing the tops of other people's heads. Any closer, we would be unable to see the full screen. Row three is the perfect distance to truly experience floating through the universe.

Through our 3-D glasses, the Space Station looks like a huge sparkplug. Or, a robotic dragonfly. It's both beautiful and ugly, mechanical and a miracle. Inside, as I float past other space sailors, I feel giddy. I wear red, white, and blue socks. My hair hovers above my head, I do somersaults in midair and sleep in a cocoon that hangs from the ceiling. When I'm thirsty, I release a wiggly ball of water into the air and catch it with my mouth.

I feel elated. Fearless. I don't want the experience to end.

At that moment, in the darkness, I understand Perry in a way I've never understood him before. Now, I know why his focus is so often out of this world. In space, nothing feels the same. Even though you are a tiny speck in a boundless universe, in space, you don't feel small. You feel *invincible*.

Sliding my 3-D glasses off my face, I turn my head and gaze at the boy beside me. But he doesn't notice. Perry Gould is lost in space—exactly where he's always wanted to be.

As soon as we get out of the theater, Perry is a kid on Christmas morning, a jackpot winner after the third seven appears on the pay line, an astronaut who takes his first step on Mars. He darts through the crowded main hall of the National Air and Space Museum, mouth dangling open, curls bobbing on top of his head, desperate to take in as much as he can before we have to leave.

"The Lunar Rover! *Apollo Eleven* Command Module!"

As cool as the IMAX film is, the museum itself is almost as awesome. Planes hang from the ceiling, a space suit stands in a corner, moon rocks are right there to hold in the palm of your hand. Perry rushes from exhibit to exhibit, aircraft to spacecraft.

"The primate space capsule!"

I rush alongside him, as thrilled as he is. My cheeks are pink. Again, I can't stop smiling. Suddenly, in a corner of the Lunar Exploration exhibit, Perry stops. He faces me, holding one shoulder in each hand. My eyes gets wide. He leans close. I see his chest rising with each breath. I feel heat radiating from his shirt. My heart catapults into my throat.

"This," he says matter-of-factly, "is a perfect day. And you, Ruthie Bayer, are a perfect girl."

WHO CARES WHAT TIME IT IS? PERRY JUST CALLED ME A
Perfect Girl. I can't wipe the smile off my face. I tried. But
I can't.

We race around the museum until the last possible
moment.

"We have to go," I say, groaning.

"Five more minutes?"

"We can't."

"We must!"

I take a deep breath, look at my watch, and say, "I'm sorry, Perry, but we have to leave *now*. If we don't, we'll never make it home."

Our Perfect Day is coming to an end.

Back out in the warm, humid D.C. air, we sprint down the museum steps. Perry is whooping and hollering across the lawn. Me, I'm bounding like a gazelle, feeling graceful and light. Just as we reach the escalator leading down to the metro, Perry stops and says, "No way."

"No way what?"

"No way can we spend our last few minutes in this awesome city underground!"

My smile fades. "We have to be at the Greyhound terminal in less than fifteen minutes. How else can we get there?"

"We fly!"

Grabbing my hand, Perry pulls me toward the Capitol Building and the bus station beyond it. His big shirt flaps in the air, his wide pants billow. *Thank God I wore sneakers,* I think, as I race beside him.

"Wa-wa*hoo!*" he yelps again. I've never seen him more alive. I've never felt more alive myself. We run and run. My chest is on fire. My body feels like a rope burn. Still, I don't want to change a single moment. The whole way, Perry never lets go of my hand.

Clearly, I need to exercise more because, with five blocks and five minutes left to go, I completely run out of gas.

"One minute," I gasp. "I. Can't. Run. Any. More."

Sweaty, red-faced, and wheezing, I involuntarily crumple to the steps of the Capitol Building. Perry folds to the ground beside me. The Capitol looms over us like a giant mushroom cloud. Unable to move, we sit there, panting, staring up.

It's a strange sensation to see something you've seen a million times before in photographs. It's ordinary, yet totally new, as if I'd only dreamed it before. My mind flashes on that night up on Perry's roof. *Thwang* night. I felt then as I do now. While gazing at something so familiar, I'm seeing it for the very first time. There on the marble steps, we're puny in front of the huge white building. But, with Perry at my side, I feel invincible.

"I can make it now," I say, clambering to my feet.

"You sure?"

"I'm sure."

Even though Perry stands, neither one of us moves. The clock is ticking, but we don't take a step. We stare up at the Rotunda, our mouths slightly open. I'm aware that we're almost out of time. But, I *feel* like time is standing still. It's as if we're in a parallel universe. Just Perry and me and our two hearts beating.

Suddenly, like some inner marionette controls us, Perry turns to me at the same instant I turn to him. Time stops completely. My body jingles like a giant wind chime. My heart *thwangs*. It's now or never. I'm ready. Our new loop is ready to begin.

"Perry," I say quietly.

"Ruthie," he says back, even softer.

My breath shallow now, I shut my eyes and tilt my head up. I wait. And wait some more. I practically send out an engraved *lip*vitation.

Slowly, the way a Polaroid develops, I begin to see the situation clearly. Blurry shapes sharpen around the edges. Faces suddenly have features. My entire existence comes into view. *What are you doing, Ruthie?* I scream in my head. Who tilts her head back, puckers her lips, and *waits* for a boy to decide he wants her?! Is this the fifties? Are we in the Stone Age? Am I my *mother*?

"Perry!" I bark. His eyeballs get white, he looks scared. I don't care. I grab Perry Gould's face and plant a *girlfriend* kiss smack on his lips. Right there on the Capitol steps.

"So there," I say, when *I'm* finished. "What do you think about that?"

He pulls back, stunned. Then he leans in. And Perry Gould plants a *boyfriend* kiss on me.

What do you think about *that*?

AS WE SPEED TOWARD THE BUS STATION, MY MIND RACES
faster than my feet. Not that I have experience or anything,
since Perry is my first boyfriend and that was my first bona
fide lip lock, but wasn't the Earth supposed to move? If not
actually move, then rattle a little? As I run for the bus, I can't
shake the sense that Perry's kiss seemed *so* much better in my

160

fantasies. The reality of it is . . . how can I put it? Way *too* real.

"There's our bus!" I screech.

Waving our arms frantically, the bus driver stops just after he pulls away from the curb.

"Thank you, thank you," I gasp, as we fly up the stairs and give the driver our tickets. "You saved our lives," I tell him.

Still panting, Perry and I find two seats near the rear and settle in for the long ride home. Neither one of us says a word.

My head is swimming.

While I hadn't expected to be transported to nirvana by the simple touch of Perry's lips (well, yeah, I *had*), I *really* hadn't counted on wondering how we'd make it home if we missed the bus. I hadn't planned on thinking about train schedules while my brand-new boyfriend planted a kiss on my lips. No way am I an expert, but I'm quite sure that a first romantic kiss is not "pleasant" in the way a ham sandwich is pleasant when you expected turkey, or as exciting as finding a quarter in the cushions of the couch.

Not that Perry did anything wrong. His kiss was the ideal balance between firm and mush, spit and dry, a little tongue action without forcing me to swallow an eel. But I felt absolutely nothing. The loop change from "friend" to

161

"boyfriend" felt absolutely *wrong*. We just had a b.f.–g.f. kind of kiss and, as much as I wished, hoped, truly, honestly, and sincerely wanted it not to be true, my heart stopped *thwanging*. Instead, it told me that Perry Gould would always be one of my very best *friends*.

How am I going to let him in on the news?

"Perry, I—" I try to swallow, but my mouth has gone dry.

"White dwarf," he says.

"Huh?"

"Is a white dwarf star brighter or dimmer than the sun?"

He pulls his iQuest out of the huge pocket in his huge pants.

"Perry—"

"You don't know?"

I stare blankly. "Dimmer?"

"Exactly. White dwarfs are about one thousand times less bright than the sun. Supergiants, the biggest stars in the known universe, can be a million times brighter than the sun."

I just look at him. He looks back at me. We have a *moment*. But in this moment, without a word, everything that needs to be said is said. *Who says words are the only way to communicate?* Perry's eyes let me know that everything is okay. He knows what I know—our kiss was a blip on the radar. An unidentified flying object. Nothing more than that. Things are flying smoothly again. We're back to normal. Apparently, Perry felt nothing, too. Or maybe he realizes the same thing I do—the way we are is the way we're supposed to be.

IT'S PRECISELY SIX FIFTEEN WHEN THE BUS PULLS INTO Wilmington. It takes another fifteen minutes to disembark and make our way through the station to the city bus stop out front. A twenty-minute ride to Odessa and we'll be home. Before seven. Just as I told my mother I would be.

The line of people waiting for the red line bus grows from five to ten. The minute hand on my watch swings past

164

twenty minutes, then twenty-five. I search the street for the bus but don't see it.

"This bus is never on time," the lady next to me says.

Panic distorts my voice. "I told my mom I'd be home at seven. It's almost seven!"

"What are ya gonna do?" she asks the air.

Perry looks at me and shrugs. Then he walks out in the street and peers down the road. He doesn't see anything, but he says, "It'll be here any minute."

The lady beside us just chuckles.

Between flashes of panic, I'm furious. We make it all the way back to Wilmington on time, and *now* we're going to be late?

Suddenly, Aunt Marty's cell rings from inside my backpack. I freeze.

"Should I get that?" I ask Perry, my stomach in spasm.

"How should I know?"

It rings again.

"Quick! Help me think of an excuse," I say. "Why am I late?"

Perry blinks. "The bus hasn't come yet."

I glare at him. He frowns at me. The phone rings again. Steeling myself, I fish it out of my backpack, press the SEND button, and say, "Hello?"

"Where are you?" Aunt Marty's voice is flat. Emotionless.

"The bus is late. I'm in Wilm—"

"Get home as soon as you can, Ruth."

"I don't know when the bus—"

"Just come home." Then she hangs up.

My armpits instantly release a flood. "I'm so dead."

"What did she say?"

"She called me *Ruth*. Aunt Marty never calls me Ruth. I'm going to be grounded for life. I'm deader than dead."

The exhilaration I'd felt all day drains out of my body like air from a punctured bicycle tire. Perry reaches his hand up and pats my shoulder.

Ten minutes later, the bus pulls up. Twenty minutes after that, it stops in Odessa. By the time Perry and I say good-bye, it's closer to seven thirty than seven. I feel flattened and wobbly.

"It was *so* worth it," Perry says.

Yeah, his mother isn't about to break the sound barrier in his ear. Kissing Perry on the *cheek*, I turn to leave. He grabs my arm.

"Ruthie?"

"Yeah?"

I face Perry Gould head-on.

"You're my best friend," he says.

For a nanosecond, the world falls away. We're two space sailors, home from our mission. That's all that counts.

"I know," I say. "I'm glad."

I don't want to open the front door. My hand hovers at the knob until I hear voices inside and figure they'll soon hear the blood throbbing through my temples. Taking a deep breath, deciding to *act* fearless, I open the door and walk in.

"Ruth." Aunt Marty stands in the center of the living room. Her messed-up hair and red-rimmed eyes instantly let me know I'm in big trouble.

"Is that my daughter?" Mom calls out from the kitchen.

I open my mouth and let the words tumble out as soon as Mom walks into the room. "I'm so sorry. Aunt Marty had nothing to do with it. It's totally my fault. Don't blame her. Punish me. It's not her fault. I swear."

Mom looks as haggard as Aunt Marty does.

"I'll do anything to make it up to you, Mom, anything. I'll do laundry, the dish—"

"Ruthie." Mom moves close to me, puts both arms around my shoulders, and gently says, "Mr. Arthur died today."

My legs suddenly feel like oatmeal. My mother and her sister rush to my side just as my knees hit the floor.

MOM WON'T GET OUT OF BED. I HADN'T REALIZED HOW
much she cared for Mr. Arthur until he was no longer there
to care about. Me, either. His absence is almost a visible
hole. I can't remember when he wasn't hanging around.
Which, I think, is why Mom is so incredibly sad. Mr.
Arthur would never leave her. Until now.

Aunt Marty brings my mother Little Debbie crumb cakes and orange spice tea. She gathers damp wads of used Kleenex and throws them away. She wipes her sister's face with a cool wet washcloth and rocks her while she sobs.

Mostly, I feel numb. I listen to CDs, set the table, do my homework, make room in the refrigerator for all the food that keeps arriving, but I'm detached from it all. Like I'm floating above me, watching myself do stuff.

"How is your mother doing?" Mrs. Fannerife asks, holding a casserole dish.

"She's okay," I say.

Mr. Perwit, our next-door neighbor, shows up with a bowl of peaches from his backyard tree.

"Is your mom hanging in there?" he asks.

"Yeah," I say.

The truth is, I'm not sure how anyone is doing. The real world seems miles away from anything I recognize. I keep waiting to rejoin myself.

In the days following his passing, I learn more about Mr. Arthur than I ever knew while he was alive. Though I should have guessed, he doesn't have *anyone* but us. The possessions in his room fill two big boxes. That's it. And, his *last* name is Arthur. His first name is Randolf, and his middle name is Eugene. Randolf Eugene Arthur had asked to be cremated and have his ashes sprinkled at the base of Mom's yellow Towne and Country rosebushes.

"Henry? I need the name of a caterer willing to come to Odessa."

After Mr. Arthur died, I learn a lot about my aunt Marty, too. She is the woman you want by your side when the world turns upside down.

When she's not comforting my mother, Aunt Marty is on the phone.

"How many lilies can you get?"

"Do they have *cushioned* white folding chairs?"

When I get home from school, I ask what I can do to help. She says, "Make sure your mother drinks a lot of water."

"Water?"

"Crying dehydrates you."

While I refill my mother's bedside water glass, Aunt Marty hires a caterer to set up a buffet table of smoked salmon and cream cheese toast points, dumplings with Asian dipping sauce, mini turkey sandwiches with country mustard, mushroom caps stuffed with lentil purée, fruit shish kebabs, coffee cake, tiny lemon tarts, coffee, tea—caf and decaf.

Aunt Marty rents chairs and has the florist in Middletown decorate a trellis in white lilies. She finds a smiling photograph of Mr. Arthur among the few things he has in his room and takes it to a twenty-four-hour print shop in Dover so they can blow it up to poster size. She speaks to the coroner about Mr. Arthur's body, strips his bed, and packs up his stuff. She interviews Mrs. Fannerife, the woman who lives above Taylor's, Mrs. Latanza of the Homeowner's Association, our neighbor Mr. Perwit, and everyone else who'd known Mr. Arthur for years, then writes his obituary and places it in the paper. Quietly, Aunt Marty takes care of every last detail.

Most important, she postpones the Peach Blossom Parade. Without Mr. Arthur as the Grand Marshal, nobody feels much like marching, anyway.

That week, I learn what a true Goddess is.

Mr. Arthur's memorial service is held in our backyard, exactly a week after he died. Everyone in town shows up, even people from Middletown and Leipsic. Even Mr. Shabala from the Wawa.

Walter Maynard and his parents arrive with Mr. Perwit. Right behind them are the Latanzas; Fire Chief Rankin; my science teacher, Mr. Galloway; and his wife. Mr. Sheeak appears with Kyle. Frankie comes with her parents and little brother. Mrs. Fannerife hands me a bouquet of flowers; the Serranos bring a coffee cake from the bakery near Pathmark.

"I won't leave your side," Celeste whispers in my ear, clutching my arm. Frankie steps up and says, "Me, neither."

Aunt Marty has turned Mom's garden into an outdoor chapel. Cushioned white chairs are arranged in neat rows on the driveway. The walkway leading to her stone bench is lined with lit white candles; Mr. Arthur's photo poster sits on an easel beneath the lily-covered trellis. It's beautiful. A small white podium is set up on the side of the bench where mourners can stand and speak. Behind that, a woman in a long, flowing blue dress plays the flute.

"How is your mom?" Mr. Galloway approaches me and rests his hand on my shoulder.

"She's okay." I offer my standard answer. "She'll be down in a minute," I add, hoping it's true.

That morning, Mom promised to pull herself together, but it was Aunt Marty who came into my room to help me figure out what to wear and what to say.

"You don't have to drape yourself in black," Aunt Marty said. "You want to honor Mr. Arthur by dressing appropriately for his final good-bye. Pick something simple and sub-dued."

Aunt Marty wears a sleeveless eggplant-colored dress and flat black shoes. I wear the only thing I have that feels right: a navy-blue shift I'd bought on sale, and a blue cotton blazer Mom bought me for the first day of school that looked too Prince William to wear any other time.

"Perfect!" Aunt Marty said that morning, which was exactly what I needed to hear.

"What am I supposed to say about him?" I'd asked her.

Aunt Marty sat me down. "Think about what you

remember most about Mr. Arthur. It doesn't have to be monumental. It just has to be *your* memory that you share with all the people who will come to remember him with you."

That, I felt I could do.

"Hi, Ruthie." Perry and his mother walk up to me while I stand with Celeste and Frankie. Perry is wearing black pants that actually fit him, a white shirt, and a narrow black tie that seems so old-fashioned it probably belonged to his dad. He looks so sweet I nearly burst into tears.

"How is your mother holding up?" Mrs. Gould asks me.

"She's okay."

Mrs. Gould nods, squeezes my arm, and takes a seat in the second row, leaving me standing between my *three* best friends.

"Hey," Perry says to Celeste and Frankie.

"Hey," they reply.

Nobody says anything else.

Isn't it weird, I think, *how you can be gone in one second and still act so jerky while you're here?*

The flutist continues to play. I wonder if my mother is ever going to come out. At that moment, Aunt Marty emerges from the house and walks up to the podium. By the way some neighbors stare and grin, I can tell they are still starstruck over Martine.

Frankie asks, "Is she going to redecorate your room, too?"

Perry rolls his eyes. He leans close to me and says, "Tonight is ideal for viewing Saturn. If you want to hang out."

"I'll be home, Ruthie, if you want to spend the night," Celeste says, giving Perry a nasty look.

I find myself cracking a smile. Things are normal in one area at least. My friends are still in the same old loop.

Up at the podium, Aunt Marty says, "Could everyone please take a seat."

Perry sits next to his mom; Celeste and Frankie sit on either side of me. Mr. Arthur's service begins while my mother is still inside the house.

"Fay has asked me to thank all of you for coming today," Aunt Marty says. "We're here to remember Randolf Eugene Arthur, a man I've been lucky enough to come to know in the past few weeks. Mr. Arthur, as everyone called him, didn't want a religious ceremony. So we're here to remember his life and say good-bye."

Suddenly, with a creak, the screen door opens. My mother steps out into the garden. Everyone turns to look. She's wearing her best dress—a chocolate-brown linen sheath she bought on sale the same day I got my navy-blue dress. I hurry over to her, escort her to the front row. Frankie moves sideways one seat, and my mom sits on my left, with Celeste on my right.

"Are you all right?" Mom quietly asks me.

"Me?"

At that moment, I realize my mother is the first person to ask how *I* am doing. Everyone else has asked about her. How *am* I doing? I don't have an answer. Since Mr. Arthur died, I've been walking around in a fog. School is almost over, my heart has stopped *thwang*ing, my mom and her sister are becoming friends, everything is changing. I feel both excited and sad. The way I feel when I hear the sound of a train in the distance. It's the sound of leaving *and* arriving. Saying good-bye so you can say hello.

Only now, it's beginning to sink in that the old man who has always been there will always be gone. It makes me feel . . . feel . . . *guilty.* I've always treated him like the weird guy who rents the third floor. But he always treated my mom and me like his family. Which I guess we were. A family of misfits living under one crumbling roof.

"I don't know how I'm doing," I say to my mom.

She nods, squeezes my hand.

At the podium, Aunt Marty continues. "Fay would like to invite anyone who wants to remember Mr. Arthur to step up and say a few words."

With that, she sits on the other side of Frankie. The flutist begins again. And no one budges. Were they waiting for the "family" to go first? As if reading my mind, Aunt Marty gives me a little nod. Before I can move, Mr. Perwit rises and walks up to the podium.

"He was a real gentleman," he says. "They don't make fellows like him anymore. That's all I have to say."

Walter Maynard stands up next. "He was always nice to me when I saw him in town."

Mr. Galloway says, "He was a walking encyclopedia. You could ask him anything about Delaware and he knew it. I've never met anyone who loved his state, and his city, more."

One by one, our neighbors, Mr. Arthur's friends, walk up to the podium. In between memories of Mr. Arthur, there's more flute music.

Kendra, the counter girl at Odessa Pizza, says, "He was a generous tipper. And funny. I always loved when he came in because he made me laugh."

"You could count on a smile when Mr. Arthur passed you in the street," says Mrs. Galloway. "He was never in a bad mood."

"He loved Odessa at Christmastime, that's for sure," Mrs. Latanza says. "For the entire month of December, Mr. Arthur was lit up like Main Street."

Mom nods and smiles.

I sit there, amazed. Why hadn't I noticed what everyone else had?

Doralee, the hairstylist at Odessa Cut 'n Curl, steps up next.

"He was a great listener. When I cut his hair, *I* did most

176

of the talking." Then she added, "And if you had fewer items than he had, he always let you go ahead in the check-out line at Pathmark."

In unison, the group nods.

Mrs. Serrano walks up to the front to say, "I never knew Mr. Arthur, but my daughter, Celeste, always came home with some interesting fact about Delaware whenever she spent time at the Bayers'."

Celeste bobs her head up and down. Perry stands up and says, "Yeah, he was cool." Then he falls back into his seat and stares at the grass.

I'm stunned that so many people have nice things to say about a man I'd lived with almost all of my life but barely knew.

As the stream of neighbors continues, my mother stares straight ahead. I stare at Mr. Arthur's blown-up photograph. I remember him asking me, "Did you know that the word 'loss' comes from the same root as the words 'to set free'?"

"No, I didn't," I'd said absentmindedly, planning an escape route.

"Yep," he'd said. "When one door shuts, another opens."

Suddenly, I become aware that Aunt Marty is looking at me again. The podium is empty. Flute music fills the air. It's time.

Heart thumping, I stand up. My black loafers feel like clown shoes as I attempt a graceful approach to the podium, still not sure exactly what to say. *What do you remember?* I hear Aunt Marty's voice in my head. *It doesn't have to be monumental.* The music stops the moment I turn to face the crowd.

"Mr. Arthur loved oatmeal."

Everyone laughs. I blush purple.

"What I mean is, he ate hot oatmeal every morning and it fogged his glasses and he went temporarily blind. Every morning without fail. Which is what I've been thinking about since he died."

I inhale, blow it out, see Odessa's eyes staring at me.

"I've been thinking how a person is formed by little things, daily things they do and say that add up to a whole being. *That's* what people remember about you. And I remember that Mr. Arthur never once said anything mean or hateful about anyone in all the time he lived with us—which is almost all my life."

Celeste brushes a fallen leaf off her lap. Mrs. Latanza clutches a handkerchief in her fist.

"I guess the biggest thing I remember about him was his kindness to me, even though I sort of ignored him."

Mom gazes at me and smiles. I smile back. Then I look at all the faces in front of me. My whole town. My whole life. I feel my knees wobble, and grab the podium to steady myself. No one makes a sound. They wait for me to speak. I wait for me to speak, too. But, all of a sudden, as if hit by a huge ball of wool, I'm startled by a thought that pops into my head: For fourteen years, I've focused on what I *don't* have—a father, a cool mother, a happening hometown, a boyfriend, the moves of a Goddess. Mr. Arthur wasn't the only person who was temporarily blind.

"Are you okay?" Aunt Marty appears at my side and whispers in my ear.

Now I know the true answer to that question.

"I will be," I say. She sits down while I elongate my neck, stand up straight, and continue. "Mr. Arthur did one thing better than anyone I've ever met—besides my mother. He *stayed*."

Sadly, it took Mr. Arthur's absence for me to finally appreciate his presence.

"That's all I have to say." With that, I sit in the front row next to my mom and let her hold my hand without freaking out even once.

A few more neighbors speak before I feel a rustling beside me. Mom blows her nose, smoothes her dress over her knees, rises, and walks to the front. The crowd goes silent.

"As most of you know," my mother begins, her voice surprisingly clear and strong, "Mr. Arthur lived with us nearly twelve years. He was a good friend. And, you're right, Mr. Perwit, he was a real gentleman. It's true, too, that he knew all about Odessa and loved to teach people about the history of the town he loved. He also taught me how to prune a rosebush, how to sun-dry tomatoes, when to hold twelve in blackjack."

A chuckle bounces through the air. Mom smiles gently. "This past week, I've come to realize that Mr. Arthur taught me the one lesson I've needed to learn for years. He taught me what *family* means."

The word *family* hangs in the air like the Goodyear blimp. Since Mr. Arthur died, I've been thinking about family, too. About my dad. I'd never be at his funeral. Could you even call yourself a "family" if the only thing your father ever gave you was his DNA?

"The day before he passed," Mom goes on, "Mr. Arthur and I were sitting right here in this garden. He told me that the one true thing he'd learned about family was that it didn't have much to do with blood. 'Family,' he said, 'are the folks who stand by you when you don't realize you can't stand by yourself.' "

Mom looks directly at Aunt Marty with tears in her eyes.

"I've been a fool," she says so softly it's less than a whisper. Still, Aunt Marty and I both hear her clearly. Amazingly, I *see* her clearly, too. For the first time ever, I see a woman who has been hurt by life, a *person* who's trying to figure out who she is and how she fits in. Just like me.

Mom says, "For opening my eyes, and for the many years Mr. Arthur was a kind, gentle member of our family, I will forever be grateful."

As I look at my mother standing there—the woman I've spent a lifetime trying not to be—I'm shocked to feel what I'm feeling. There, before my very eyes, my own mother morphs into a pretty cool person after all.

ODESSA, LIKE MOST SMALL TOWNS, LOVES A PARADE. IT'S
hilarious, when you think about it. The same people we've
known all our lives march down the Main Street we see
every day, past the houses everyone lives in. Most people are
in the parade so there aren't a lot of watchers and wavers.
Which is why Mom and I have always stood on the sidelines. For Mr. Arthur. So he had someone to march *for.*

This year, three weeks after Mr. Arthur's memorial, after school is out and summer has begun, the Peach Blossom Parade is back on. It's the way he would have wanted it.

Mr. Perwit was elected the new Grand Marshal of the Peach Blossom Parade. Well, not *elected* in the true definition of the word. He volunteered and nobody said no.

The day before the parade, Mr. Sheeak and Kyle tied orange ribbons around the Dutch elms along Main Street. Walter Maynard and other kids from the Liberty High School Marching Band shined up their instruments. Mr. Galloway distributed sprigs of peach blossoms for the onlookers to wave. And Mrs. Fannerife baked chocolate chip cookies to sell. She had intended to bake miniature peach cobblers, she said, but she overslept.

Around ten in the morning, on parade day, Mom, Aunt Marty, and I join the whole town—and much of Middletown—at the firehouse. Chief Rankin stands at the huge stove making pancakes for twenty-five cents each. The smell of vanilla and melted butter fills the air.

I see her right away. Jenna.

Dressed in a light orange skirt and white T-shirt, she looks like tangerine sorbet and whipped cream. She looks . . . *perfect.*

"Fresh peach nectar!" Mrs. Latanza has set up a card table near the entrance and sells juice for a buck a cup. A cardboard sign taped to the table reads, ALL PROCEEDS BENEFIT THE ODESSA HOMEOWNER'S ASSOCIATION. While Aunt

Marty and I get in the pancake line, Mom buys juice.

"Gorgeous day, isn't it, Peg?" Mom opens her purse and pulls out three dollars.

Mrs. Latanza's jaw drops. "Fay, what have you done to yourself?"

"A little makeover," Mom says.

Truthfully, I was stunned, too. A few days earlier, after we sprinkled Mr. Arthur's ashes at the base of Mom's rose-bushes, my mother disappeared into her bathroom. I thought she was crying. But she wasn't. She was dyeing her hair Auburn Sunset.

"Time for a change." That's all she said to us when she finally came out.

That morning, Mom blew her curls dry into soft, flattering waves. Her lips now glisten with ginger-colored gloss. Soft brown shadow deepens her eyes. She tossed out her velour pantsuits for good.

"Martha must be behind this," says Mrs. Latanza.

Mom laughs. "Yeah, I guess she is."

Scooping up all three cups of juice, Mom joins Aunt Marty and me at the long dining table in the firehouse kitchen. Our three stacks of cakes smell delicious.

The scene is achingly familiar. My mother, Mr. Arthur, and I have eaten pancakes at this same firehouse table every year, for as long as I can remember. It's always been the same scene. But not this year.

Celeste and her parents walk in as I'm soaking up the

last pool of syrup with my last forkful of pancakes. She smiles and waves. I wave back. Frankie isn't here yet, but I know she will be. For the first time, the sense of sameness, of knowing exactly what to expect, doesn't feel like a tight turtleneck choking me.

I *sense* him before I see him. He comes in through the side door. Which is *so* like him. Perry, like my aunt Marty, never does anything the ordinary way. His whole being resembles a ripe peach. Fuzzy light hair on his upper lip, pink cheeks.

"Yo, Bayer." He nods in my direction, stands in the pancake line, and forklifts a dollar's worth of pancakes onto his plate. Jenna Wilson, in her tangerine outfit, makes a beeline for him.

Mrs. Gould, Perry's mom, enters through the front, buying two cups of peach juice on her way to the firehouse table. She sets Perry's juice at the far end of the table. Perry joins her, carrying three plates of pancakes. One for him, one for his mom, one for Jenna.

My heart breaks a little. Not so much for what is—or what's *about* to be—but for what will have to wait. My heart aches for the time I'll look at someone the way Jenna Wilson now looks at Perry Gould. And the way he looks at her.

"Ruthie!" Frankie bounds over. "Save me a seat!"

The sizzle of pancakes on the firehouse grill, the squeals of Odessa's kids, the sight of Perry's pink cheeks, Mom's pretty hair, Aunt Marty's white teeth, warm memories of Mr. Arthur, and the cool sensation of my delicious-secret underpants make me feel happy to be right where I belong: in Odessa, Delaware, with everyone I love.

A trumpet blast announces the beginning of the parade. Mr. Perwit leaps to his feet and shouts, "Follow me, Odessans!" just as Mr. Arthur had for the past gazillion years. Wiping the syrup from their chins, the whole town stands and follows.

Suddenly, Mom yells, "Wait!"

I stop. Everyone else stops, too. Stunned, we watch my mother race out the back door of the firehouse.

"Where is she going?" Mr. Galloway asks me.

I have no idea.

Mrs. Fannerife whispers, "Perhaps she needs to use the little girls' room." Then she adds, "I don't like to use anyone else's restroom, either."

As suddenly as she disappeared, Mom reappears, breathless, holding a shopping bag. She opens it and pulls out a hat. Everyone applauds.

Years ago, Mom knit Mr. Arthur a peach-colored top hat to wear in the parade. And every year, he wore it perched on top of his head, at the front of the parade, while he pumped the Grand Marshal's scepter like an oil derrick.

"He would want you to have it," Mom says, as she places the freshly washed hat on Mr. Perwit's (unfortunately, much smaller) head. "So do I."

Mr. Perwit whirls around, the peach top hat settling comically on his ears. Holding the scepter high, he shouts, "Now, follow me, Odessans!"

Happily, we all strut outside.

It seems to be over as soon as it begins. The marching band barely finishes one round of "Our Delaware" before Mr. Perwit reaches the end of Main Street. He circles around and marches straight back to the firehouse, the band's military formation not surviving the turn. Celeste, Frankie, and five other girls from Middletown jiggle pom-poms in the parade. Toddlers waddle behind them wearing stuffed orange pillowcases sewn into round peach shapes. Most of them wander off to the sidelines as soon as they spot their parents.

Bringing up the rear, like a Barbie doll and her Ken, are Jenna and Perry. Both are smiling. Jenna waves. They walk together, awkwardly, but somehow in sync.

"Are you okay?" Aunt Marty asks me softly, watching me watch Perry.

I surprise myself with the answer.

"Yeah," I say. Looking at Perry fills me with a longing for someone *else*. Someone truly right for me. Seeing Perry with Jenna confirms the feeling: Perry Gould will always be one of my very best friends. Amazingly, that's okay.

Suddenly, as if my legs are moving on their own, I leap

forward and jump into the parade. It's almost over, but I don't care. I run to the front, to Celeste and Frankie. Frankie hands me one of her pom-poms and I wave it wildly over my head. My knees pump up and down as I march. I hold my head up and grin. My heart feels light.

When one door shuts, another opens.

WE HAVE ONE LAST FAMILY DINNER—THE THREE OF US.
Aunt Marty cooks. She slices a head of cauliflower like a loaf
of bread, brushes each piece with olive oil, sprinkles them
with salt and pepper, then roasts all the slices in the oven on
a cookie sheet. For "spice" she grills scallops that have been
marinated in a chipotle vinaigrette. When arranged on
plates, our dinner looks like three scrumptious flowers.

"Wow." It's all we can say. Who knew vegetables could taste so good?

The next morning, my mother and I say good-bye to the woman who changed our lives.

"Do you have to go?" I ask Aunt Marty.

"I can't hide in Delaware forever." She cups my chin the same way she did on the day she arrived.

"It's worked for me," Mom jokes.

The three of us laugh. My mother actually looks pretty standing next to her sister. And Aunt Marty is as gorgeous as ever. Even though she'll be moving into a much smaller apartment and—she insists—a much smaller life, my aunt Marty is every bit the goddess she will always be.

"Thank you for the furniture," Mom says, "and our colorful walls. I'll pay you back."

"You don't have to pay me back, Fay. I don't need that stuff anymore. Besides, we're *family*, remember?"

"Still . . ." Mom's voice trails off. I know what she's thinking. She owes her sister so much. How can she *ever* repay her? How can I?

"I'm only three hours away," she says, her voice quavering. "Three seconds by phone."

Aunt Marty throws her arms around my mother and squeezes. "I love you, Fay."

"I love you, too," Mom says. Then she adds, "My beautiful sister."

With tears running down her cheeks (though her

makeup somehow remains *perfect*), Aunt Marty turns to me.

"Lovely Ruthie," she says.

We hug each other hard. I stand there and feel her heart beating into mine. The sense that she will always be part of my family fills me with joy. Tilting my head up, I whisper, "Thank you." But it sounds unbearably lame. How can you thank someone for showing you yourself? Where you belong, the potential for who you can become?

"My darling," Aunt Marty whispers back, "thank me by being *you*."

Funny, that's exactly what I plan to do.

IT'S THE HOTTEST SUMMER I CAN REMEMBER. MY ARMS are dotted with mosquito bites. I can't bear the feel of heavy hair on my neck. I'm tempted to cut it all off, but Celeste and Frankie stop me by saying, "Winter will come *way* before your hair grows back."

They have a point. So I pile it all on top of my head every morning and hold it there with a claw clip. I hang out in Dover Mall as often as Mom will let me—which is much more often than she used to (thank you, Aunt Marty!)—eating Dippin' Dots and drinking Diet Cokes.

That's where the three of us are today. Mrs. Serrano drove us. A friend of hers is getting married again, and she needs to buy a gift.

"It's not fair that you should buy *three* wedding gifts just because your friend can't stay married to one guy," Celeste said on the way to the mall.

"I don't mind," Mrs. Serrano said. "Sometimes it takes a few tries to get it right."

See how cool she is?

"Meet me here in three hours," Mrs. Serrano says to us at the Information Booth. We nod and wave and disappear into the swarm of shoppers.

"Where to?" I ask my best friends.

"Let's just walk," Frankie says.

We do. The cool air smells of cinnamon and butter. A strand of hair falls out of my clip, but I don't care. I'm happy to hang with my friends and wander through the mall looking at mannequins and picturing myself in their clothes. Just like a normal girl.

Club Monaco is having a sale. Not that I have any money. Still, I stare at the white-and-black window display and imagine a day when I'll walk in and pluck a shirt off the rack without even looking at the price ta—

"S'cuse me," a male voice mutters.

A guy bumps into me as he rounds the corner. His shoulder brushes against mine, and we lock gazes for a moment. Long enough for me to notice his blue eyes and spiky hair. Celeste sneers at him and we keep walking. He keeps walking, too. But, a few steps later, I turn and see that he has turned around, too. One of his friends tugs his sleeve, but he stares at me and smiles. I grin and blush.

"Come *on*, Ruthie," Celeste says.

Another strand of my hair falls softly onto my face. Tucking it behind my ear, I ask, "You guys hungry?"

Frankie says, "Starved."

"Me, too."

"Me, three," I say.

We step on the escalator up to the food court. It's early, not too crowded. There are only two people ahead of us in the Dippin' Dots line.

"Low-fat vanilla, please," I tell the clerk. "Small."

"I'll try Rootbeer Float," says Celeste.

Frankie tries the orange sorbet.

Sitting near the edge of the food court, we prop our feet up on three chairs and feel the dots melt in our mouths and slither down our throats.

His hair is the first thing I see. Rising up on the escalator, the short blond spikes poke up like dune grass. They become blue eyes, then tan lips, and a white T-shirt over baggy khaki shorts.

My chest feels hot even as the ice cream cools it down.

"Hey," he says to me, nodding as he passes our table.

"Hey," I say back.

Frankie asks, "Isn't that the guy who rammed into you?"

"Yeah." I smile, my heart going nuts. "It is."

Spiky Guy and his two friends get slices from Sbarro. They sit close to us. Celeste now perks up.

"I think they want to talk to us," she says, her eye on Spiky Guy's dark-haired friend.

Frankie says, "That guy with the shaggy hair is kinda cute."

I feel my blood pulse through my ears. Spiky Guy finishes the last of his pizza, stands up, runs one hand through his hair, and walks straight for me. For *me*.

"I'm Justin," he says.

I try to tell him my name, but my throat is closed.

"She's Ruthie," Celeste says, "I'm Celeste, and this is Frankie."

"Cool."

Justin stands still for a moment. He looks at his huge white sneakers. Then back at me. Celeste wipes the corner of her mouth to make sure all traces of Rootbeer Float are gone. Frankie glances over at the guy with the shaggy curls. I try not to feel the strand of hair that's now stuck to my sweaty neck. Suddenly, Justin looks as though he may leave.

"I'm from Odessa," I blurt out.

He says, "I live in Smyrna."

Smyrna is about halfway between Odessa and Dover.

"Cool," I say. Then my brain locks again. I twirl my empty Dippin' Dots cup, cross and uncross my legs. Then, I remember what I'm wearing. My own delicious secret. Tilting my head up, I breathe in and out. I elongate my neck and *act* fearless. Maybe he'll believe what he thinks he sees.

"We'll be here for a couple of hours," I say, forcing myself to look directly into Justin's eyes. "Wanna hang out?"

Celeste and Frankie both give me a look that lets me know it's okay. Justin flicks his head to invite his friends over. Without words (who needs words when you have *electricity*?!), the six of us stand and make our way down the escalator and into the mall.

"I'm Ricky," Justin's friend says. He has black eyes like Celeste's.

Shaggy Guy says, "I'm Ryan."

We all nod hello, act nonchalant. We pass Borders and the Gap. Frankie and Ryan say something about school. Celeste and Ricky talk about how dead Delaware is. But I've never felt more alive.

As we walk, Justin's bare forearm brushes against my bare forearm. It's both cool and hot. Soft and rough. He smells like the mall, like cinnamon and butter.

"I like your hair," he says.

"I like yours, too," I reply.

I smile, then discover I can't stop smiling.

All of a sudden, my insides feel like Cream of Wheat.

Thwang. Just like that.